MURDER MOST UNLUCKY

A CAROLYN NEVILLE MYSTERY BOOK 5

JOHN DUCKWORTH

Murder Most Unlucky
Print Edition
Copyright © 2021 John Duckworth

CKN Christian Publishing
An Imprint of Wolfpack Publishing
5130 S. Fort Apache Rd. 215-380
Las Vegas, NV 89148

www.cknchristianpublishing.com

Paperback ISBN 978-1-63977-096-0
eBook ISBN 978-1-64734-536-5

MURDER MOST UNLUCKY

To Christopher and Jonathan, who've made me the luckiest dad in the world.

PROLOGUE

I CHECKED THE MIRROR. "WHITE CADILLAC ABOUT A MILE behind us."

"Got it," Stephen said. "Take this next road to the right."

I let go of the steering wheel and let the car have its way.

"I'm trying not to think about what's going to happen when the rental company hears their car has burned to a crisp," I said.

Stephen snorted. "Probably will, given the full gas tank. But they won't find any bodies—unless we screw up."

"Maybe they'll think we were thrown clear and survived. They'll search for us. But they won't know we've gone to Pennsylvania."

Stephen looked at his phone. "Slow down." He paused. "Are they still behind us?"

"Yeah, about half a mile."

"Okay. There's a sharp left turn and a ravine about 300 feet ahead. We'll have to bail out before that."

I swallowed and sent up a quick prayer. Were I Catholic, I'd be grabbing my dashboard St. Christopher.

Slowing to about 15 miles per hour, I unsnapped my seatbelt and hoisted my purse on my shoulder.

"We'll have to make a run for it," Stephen said. "Into those trees on the right."

Glancing in the mirror, I saw Stuart clutching his suitcase, pale as parchment.

"I'll count down from ten," Stephen said. "Try to hit the ground running."

We were nearing the cliff. I gripped the handle of my overnight bag.

"*Three . . . two . . . one,*" Stephen said.

We flung the doors open. "*Now!*"

I rolled through the weeds, hoping I'd stop before I ran out of ground. Stuart was on my side and hit the dirt like a bale of hay.

I helped him up. Stephen was dusty but apparently unharmed.

The three of them fled toward the trees. Stuart was limping.

The car sailed over the edge, hit the rocks, and burst into flame.

CHAPTER 1

THE WEATHER AT LEGENDS OF CAMELOT MINI-GOLF WAS HOT as a ghost pepper that day. I wiped my forehead with the back of my left hand, the right being occupied with a club that didn't quite reach the ground.

Had we cared about the druthers of my boss, Hunter Thicke, we would have been torturing ourselves with Scotland's most unpalatable export, the real thing. To his way of thinking, such as it was, golf was the only way for Pendleton House Publishing to celebrate the achievement of its best-selling and most endearing children's author, Stuart Lytle. He'd built a hospital in India with ten percent of the royalties from his Jennifer Jenner mystery series. He might fund another now that Jennifer was set to become the star of an animated PBS show.

"Your shot," he said, sweating profusely and nodding at my inexplicably young senior editor, Stephen Ames. We all faced a green fiberglass dragon the height of a two-story building, breathing orange-yellow fiberglass fire, wild-eyed and spiny-tailed. Stephen, who tended to take this sort of thing much too seriously, pulled his Mets cap down over his scarlet eyebrows and took what appeared to be a professional stance. The trick would be to get the ball between the dragon's feet and into a giant fiberglass toilet bowl.

His stroke was perfect. The ball cleared the claws and dropped into the target, triggering a satisfying recorded FLOOOOSH. He pumped his fist into the air, took off his hat, and fanned his flushed and freckled face.

"Reminds me of the course in Atlantic City," he said. "They've got this windmill with a blade that spins fast as a food processor. I swear if you moved too slowly, it'd turn you to hamburger. And their skull is a hoot. Big as three NBA players standing on each other's shoulders, painted gold, with eyes that light up red. It's got a cigar in its mouth, and you're supposed to knock it out so the jaw clamps down. Never saw anybody do it. And—"

"Fascinating," I lied. "But isn't anybody else hot? Can we move this along before we get heat stroke?"

Stuart ran a pudgy hand over his spiky gray hair. "You can't rush greatness, my dear. As far as I'm concerned, this is the sport of kings."

"Actually, that's horse racing," Stephen said, still fanning himself.

Stuart, looking like a very large little kid in his baggy gray tropical shirt, black shorts, and thick, round glasses, chuckled until his oversized torso registered a 4.5 on the Richter Scale. "Fine. You've caught me in a very expansive mood. Let's wrap this up and go to the snack bar to return our putters."

As if to confirm his generosity, on the last hole he took a dive, muffing an easy shot over an elephant's trunk that moved slowly up and down and sprayed water. It was clearly on purpose, no doubt intended to make my score look less humiliating. I did, after all, have the power to insert an embarrassing multitude of unnecessary commas into his next book.

We got drinks and sat down on the uncomfortable green steel chairs at one of the sticky green tables. I looked around at the dozen or so patrons under the umbrellas, half of whom were parents staring vacantly at their hyperactive rug rats mourning the loss of the ice cream on their cones due to Nap-Deprived Clumsiness Syndrome.

"So," I said. "PBS. You've come up in the world, Stuart. I can remember when you drew cartoons on that cable access kid's show."

He sighed. "Those were the days." He leaned forward conspiratorially. "Speaking of PBS, did you know Mr. Ratburn on *Arthur* is gay?"

"Who doesn't?" Stephen asked.

Stuart looked disappointed. "Nobody tells me anything."

Stephen downed the last of his drink and surveyed the small crowd. "Huh," he said.

"What?" I asked.

He pointed at a hefty, gray-haired man three tables away, dining alone. "Does he remind you of anybody?"

"No."

"He looks like Stuart, at least from the back."

I squinted. "Not that much."

I watched as a thirtyish man in sunglasses, oily-looking, stringy brown hair askew, sidled up behind the alleged doppelgänger and put a hand on his shoulder. Within a few seconds the latter slumped into his plate.

I drew a deep breath. No one seemed to notice. The man who'd touched him slipped away toward the parking lot.

Without a word I grabbed my purse and went to the victim. There was no pulse.

I got out my phone to dial 911. No charge.

Returning to our table, I felt numb.

"Need to borrow your phone," I told Stephen.

* * *

He handed me his Samsung without looking up from his cup. Stuart was already standing, open-mouthed, apparently having seen the commotion.

"Got to get out of here," he said, backing away from the table, sweating more than ever.

"Why?" I asked, pushing the buttons on Stephen's phone.

"Is that guy *dead?*" Stephen asked.

The 911 operator answered. "We're at the Legends of Camelot mini-golf place," I said, and gave the address. "I think there's been a murder."

"Stay on the line. Are you sure the person is dead?"

"Couldn't find a pulse."

"Is anyone else in danger?"

I hesitated. According to Stuart, he could be next in line. Maybe we *all* could. But that wasn't what she meant.

"Not that I know of," I said.

"Let's *go,*" Stuart whispered.

"Police and ambulance should be there in ten minutes," the dispatcher said.

I handed the phone back to Stephen. "Now, what's this all about?"

I looked at Stuart. He looked away.

"We have a right to know," I said.

"I'll tell you in the car," he whispered, and headed for the exit.

The other patrons had retreated from the dead man's table, leaving only the clerk from the snack bar to sit, helpless, next to him.

We followed Stuart to the parking lot. He kept his head lowered as if not wanting to be recognized.

The inside of my car was doing its best imitation of a toaster oven. We shut our doors. I turned the key and pushed the A/C button. Wasn't helping yet.

Stuart gave a squeak from the back seat. "It's *him*."

"*He*," I said.

"He *who?*" Stephen asked. "Why are we—"

"Let him leave first," Stuart said, his voice muffled, face pressed against the back of my seat.

We waited. The temperature grew less volcanic at a glacial pace.

Slowly Stuart raised his head. "Okay, he's gone."

"Where are we going?" I asked, impatient.

He sagged against his seat and exhaled, deflating slowly as the last balloon in the Macy's Thanksgiving Day Parade.

"Anywhere but here."

CHAPTER 2

PENDLETON HOUSE SEEMED LIKE A SAFE PLACE TO GO, DESPITE the sometimes deadly office politics and the world's most dangerously clueless supervisor. Manhattan traffic was constipated as ever.

Stuart, seemingly unaffected by the air conditioning, loosened his collar and kept looking at the lanes on either side of us.

"Time's up," I said. "Tell us what's going on."

"Yeah," Stephen said.

"I can't."

"If you don't, I'll turn around and go back to that stupid golf course. I'm sure the police would like to ask you a few questions."

"I'll talk when we get to Hunter's office."

I hit the steering wheel with my palm. "Stuart, some mysteries are intriguing. Some are just irritating."

"Sorry," he said. "When you hear the whole story, you'll understand. Or you might just want to kill me."

* * *

Hunter was practicing putts on a small patch of artificial grass next to his desk, head down, brushed-back black hair as shiny as ever. "Just a minute," he muttered.

We waited. Stuart flopped into a chair, still sweating.

"Fore!" Hunter yelled, tapped the ball into the hole, and twirled his club like a Miss America contestant with a baton. Looking up, he smiled that serial killer smile and winked at me.

"Stuart has something to tell you," I said. "To tell all of us, actually."

Hunter turned toward him. Poor Stuart's face was pale as a butternut squash, but the boss didn't notice. "Tell me all about your game. Who won?"

"Stuart did," Stephen said. "I think he blew the elephant's trunk on purpose at the end."

Hunter looked confused. "There was an *elephant* on the course? Escaped from the zoo, or what?"

Stuart rubbed his temples with his chubby fingers. "My fault. I insisted we play *miniature* golf."

"Oh," Hunter said, obviously disappointed. Then he shrugged. "It's *your* day, Stu. You can play anything you want." He leaned his putter against a wall of shelves holding books he would probably never read.

Stuart sighed. "That's my problem. I'm a little too fond of games."

"What sort of games?" I asked.

"Games of chance." He rubbed his eyes.

A queasy sensation rose in my gut like antifreeze in an overheated radiator. "Gambling?" I asked. "As in casinos?" I asked.

He nodded, looking miserable. "I have a problem."

"Our best children's author is a *gambling* addict? How did *that* happen?"

"Slowly. I'm a man of great appetites. No excuse, I know. It started at an ABA convention in Las Vegas. I won about $350 playing craps."

"So why was that man at the snack bar after you?"

"I owe some people a little money."

"How much?"

He cleared his throat and looked away. "About two hundred thousand," he said, his voice squeaking.

"*Dollars?*" Hunter cried.

"I don't have it."

Feeling faint, I lowered myself onto the sofa across from Hunter's desk. Hunter himself sat in his chair, frozen in disbelief.

Stephen grinned. "Man, I've never met anybody who was in hock to a real live loan shark. That must be pretty exciting."

Stuart stared at him. "Do I *look* excited?"

"No," I said. "You look like a cadaver."

"You know," Stephen said, "loan sharks used to be a big business. People who owed them would pledge their bodies as collateral."

Stuart groaned.

"Fifty years ago the mob started concentrating on stuff like money laundering and gamblers. In fact, loansharking was their second biggest racket, right behind gambling itself."

I looked at my watch.

"Stuff like payday loans has made the really bad guys harder to find."

"Too bad I found one," Stuart mumbled. "A whole family, actually."

"Have they threatened to break your kneecaps?"

Stuart shook his head. "Worse. I recognized the guy who killed the man who looked sort of like me. Name's Jeremy."

I frowned. "How could he know you'd be at a miniature golf course?"

"Been following me for the last couple of months. Works for Angel Boudreaux. Threatened me over the phone."

Hunter roused himself from his stupor. "Did you call the police?"

Stuart laughed bitterly. "These people see that as impolite. Socially unacceptable." He paused. "Jeremy and I have never met in person. Maybe that explains how he could mistake that poor guy for me."

"This Angel," Stephen said. "Related to Max Boudreaux?"

"His daughter. And next in line, I hear."

Stephen whistled. "I've heard of this guy." He picked up his phone and started swiping and poking. "Born ten years after Dillinger died. They've never been able to pin anything on him, but he's probably indirectly responsible for at least a hundred killings. In his eighties now. Family lives in a mansion in New Orleans."

I wanted to take Stuart by the collar and shake him, maybe deliver a rant about the evils of vices that didn't appeal to me. But all I could manage was a sigh.

"Oh, Stuart," I said, and closed my eyes.

"I know you think this is a terrible idea," I continued. "But what's the worst that could happen if we go to the police?"

He leaned forward, clasped his hands as if in prayer, and lowered his head. "You can bet the Boudreauxs have paid off at least two or three cops. My career would be over, not to mention my life."

Stephen scratched his head. "Isn't organized crime an FBI thing?"

"Yeah, but they've never been able to pin the family on a murder charge. If I go to them, the Boudreauxs will add me to their list of canceled debtors."

Stephen went back to his phone and resumed searching. "Aha!" he said finally. "Here's an article about a guy named Robert Gallagher. Retired FBI agent, age 67."

He handed me the phone. There was Gallagher's photo. Short, tired-looking, head shaved. Apparently his purpose in life had been to bring the family down.

"That'll never happen," Stuart said. "Only thing I can do now is run."

I read further in the article. The former agent lived in someplace called Berwyn, near Chicago.

"Can you find his number?" I asked Stephen.

It took him less than two minutes. I don't know how he did it, and don't want to.

I picked up my phone and started to punch in the numbers, but Hunter's desk phone rang first. He jumped a little.

After listening for a few moments, he covered the receiver with his hand. "It's one of our friends in Security. There's a guy who wants to come up here. Claims he's a friend of yours, Stuart."

He put the phone on speaker. Stuart got up and stood by the desk.

"What does he look like?"

The guard paused. "Just a second."

There was a rustling sound. "Okay, I'm back. Don't want the guy to overhear. He's about thirty. A little greasy-looking, messed-up brown hair, bug-eyed. I didn't see it at first, but he's missing an ear. Probably makes it hard to keep his sunglasses on."

Stuart shuddered.

"You know that guy on *The Office?*" the guard continued. "The one who kept saying he was the Assistant Office Manager and glaring at everybody?"

"Dwight Schrute," Stephen volunteered. "Played by Rainn Wilson."

"Yeah. Looks kind of like him."

Panicking, Stuart shot a glance at the door.

"It's Jeremy," he said. "Too late."

CHAPTER 3

IF I HADN'T KNOWN BETTER, I'D HAVE THOUGHT HUNTER WAS one of those politically toxic concrete lawn jockeys, only taller and grayer and less lively. He sat there with the phone in his hand, mouth open slightly. It took him a good half minute to find his voice.

"Tell the guy I'm not in," he whispered, and returned the receiver to its cradle.

I rummaged through my mental map case for the blueprint of the Pendleton Building. "We've got a fire escape, right?"

Hunter nodded numbly.

"I think it's in the back," I said. "Shouldn't be too hard to get to street level. We're only on the second floor."

Stuart looked out the window and made a sound like a spaniel lamenting a lost bone. "Are you sure? Seems a lot higher than that."

"I think I should stay here," Hunter said faintly.

"Wouldn't have it any other way," I said.

Stephen rose. "Follow me,"

"Who died and made you Tom Cruise?" I asked.

He folded his arms. "I was a Boy Scout for a year. Of course, this was before they got sued over—"

"Never mind. I'm sure you earned your merit badges for Baking Potatoes in Tin Foil and Fire Escape Climbing. Go ahead."

After taking Stuart squarely by the shoulders and lining him up behind Stephen, I turned to Hunter. "We'll be in touch." He nodded like a jet-lagged Japanese tourist trying to make sense of a Brooklynite's directions to Yankee Stadium.

The three of us went down the hall, not exactly tiptoeing, which is physically impossible. I for one felt extremely stealthy, however.

Stephen stopped at the fourth window on the right. FIRE ESCAPE, said the red-on-white sign next to the casing. Grabbing the grips at the base of the sash, he yanked upward with a mighty grunt. Nothing happened, except for a possible hernia.

"Stuart, give me a hand," he said. Stuart took one handle and Stephen took the other. "On three. One . . . two . . ."

In unison, they jerked upward with barely-stifled primal screams. The sash didn't budge.

Panting, Stephen reached in his pocket. "I still carry my Scout penknife. Sometimes these windows get painted shut. I doubt anybody's opened this one in years."

He ran the blade from one side of the sill to the other, then snapped the knife shut and stuck it back in his pocket.

They tried once more, and this time the earth moved. Just an inch, and with a dry squeak of protest. I got between them and the three of us gave it one more try. This time the job got done.

I wasn't sure Stuart could get out, but we didn't have much choice. Stephen went first, ducking as low as he could and squeezing like a spelunker in a particularly nasty cave.

He ended up on the rusty metal platform, which swayed slightly but held his weight.

"Can't do it," Stuart said.

"Of course you can," I said. "I've seen you do the impossible. Remember the day your mom died? You were a mess, but you got it together and did the big reading at the Tattered Cover Bookstore. You didn't want to let those kids down."

"Yeah, I remember."

"I've seen you at your best."

"Well, this is my worst."

With a sigh he positioned his bulk in front of the portal and began to maneuver through the opening. I considered pushing his rear end, but didn't want to seem overly familiar.

Finally he emerged from the tunnel and plopped onto the platform like a sausage from an assembly line. I followed, landing a little too close to a long, rusted bolt that stuck out from the frame. I couldn't remember the last time I'd had a tetanus shot.

Stuart, dazed, sat there. He was wheezing so much I thought he might have a heart attack.

Stephen held onto the side of the escape and frowned. "Not quite as easy as I thought. More of a ladder than a staircase. But it's only about twenty feet."

"You okay?" I asked Stuart.

He shook his head.

"Good. You get too cocky about something like this and you start to make mistakes. At least that's what they say in the movies." Doubtful, but it sounded rather inspirational.

Stephen took hold of the iron-pipe railings and started descending backward, one slow step at a time. The whole contraption still swayed a little, but it was obviously going to hold. Or not.

I patted Stuart on the shoulder and helped him to his feet. Eyes wild with trepidation, he placed his shoes carefully in

Stephen's footsteps and began the journey with a slow *tap tap tap* down the stairs.

At the second switchback, he misjudged a step and found his foot dangling in midair. With a gasp, he lost his footing. His sweaty hands slid off the pipe.

I reached forward, trying to catch him, but it was too late. A strangled scream came from his throat as he plummeted to the ground. Stephen swore.

Stuart landed in a dumpster packed with trash bags. I hoped they weren't full of broken beer bottles and railroad spikes.

Still off balance from my failed rescue attempt, I missed the last rung. Flailing for a handhold that wasn't there, I looked down and saw Stuart on his back amid the garbage. His eyes grew wide as he saw me coming.

I couldn't stop myself, of course. There wasn't even time to pray.

With an *OOOF* I landed on something relatively soft. At least half of it was Stuart.

I made a mental note to thank him for breaking my fall, if he was still alive.

* * *

I tried not to breathe, the stench of rancid orange juice and wet diapers having permeated the air. I could hear Stuart groaning somewhere below me.

"Thank you," I said, wincing from the pain in my leg. "Sorry I couldn't defy the law of gravity."

The smell got worse as he tried to sit up, popping several bags open in the process. "Neither could I," he mumbled. He held his hands in front of him. "No blood."

"You sound disappointed," I said, fishing my purse from the refuse and making a mental note to soak it in bleach as soon as possible.

"Not disappointed. Just amazed."

Stephen's face appeared above the edge of the dumpster. "Anybody dead?"

"Not here," I said. Stuart made an effort to adjust his reeking clothes as we slowly climbed out.

"Keep your heads down," Stephen said.

Stuart was limping a little as we made our way back to the car, staying close to the alley walls and under the awnings. By the time we opened the car doors three blocks away, we stank like the New Fulton Fish Market when the fans break down in August.

I turned the key in the ignition, hoping Jeremy didn't know how to wire a car bomb. We all rolled the windows down.

"I'd ask where we're going," Stuart said, "but I guess we've covered that."

"Watch for that Cadillac," I said, pulling away from the curb. "And let me know if we pass a place that sells deodorant."

* * *

The coast was clear for about two miles when we happened upon a Walgreens. Running inside, I found some Secret for me and Irish Spring for the guys. The clerk wrinkled her nose, coughed, and kept her distance as I handed over the cash and gave her my Balance Rewards card.

"Yeah, I know," I said. "P.U., Sigma Nu."

Judging from the look on her face, she wasn't familiar with the phrase. She dropped the items into a bag, handed it over, and told me with obvious insincerity to have a nice day.

We stuck our respective antiperspirants into our armpits, which didn't help much. God only knew how long it would be until we found a laundromat and the time to use it.

On the road again, we spotted an old white Cadillac down the road at a gas station.

"I think we're being followed," Stephen said.

I swallowed. "You mean *preceded*."

I turned toward the pumps as we passed. Couldn't see the driver, but had to assume the worst.

Traffic was light enough that I could speed up to 20 miles per hour or so. Before I knew it, the Caddy was on our tail.

I gunned it to 23. So did he.

Peering into the rearview mirror, I couldn't make out the driver's face.

I cranked it up to 25.

He matched it.

"Most boring car chase in history," Stephen muttered. "Remember *The French Connection*? Gene Hackman races through Chicago at about 90 miles an hour. Directed by William Friedkin. They didn't even have permission to shoot there. It was a wonder nobody got killed."

The Queensboro Bridge exit was on the right. I jerked the wheel; the Caddy didn't follow.

Stuart groaned as we met a wall of traffic.

"Carolyn, we're freakin' stuck," Stephen said. "How are we supposed to get anywhere?"

"Safest place to be." Slowing to a crawl, I checked the dashboard to make sure we weren't overheating. *I* was, but our vehicle wasn't.

Stuart unbuttoned his collar and pulled his shirt up as high as he could, a turtle retreating into his shell. "Something like this happened to Jennifer Jenner, except she wasn't being chased by a guy who used a cheese grater to get answers."

Stephen made a disgusted noise. "The A/C on this car sucks."

I resisted the urge to push my seat back into his trachea. "Weren't you trying to reach that Gallagher guy? The former agent?"

He sighed and pulled out his phone. Two tries later he connected.

"Agent Gallagher?" Stephen asked.

I couldn't hear the reply.

"Yes, *former* agent. Sir, this is Stephen Ames with Pendleton Publishing. One of our authors has gotten himself in trouble with the Boudreaux family. I understand they've been your hobby for a long time."

Another pause.

"Well, maybe *hobby* isn't the right word. Anyway, three of us are in a car, trying to get out of Manhattan. We think we're being followed by a greasy-haired guy named Jeremy who works for the family. Can you help us out?"

I couldn't make out Gallagher's reply, but it sounded like a bear being poked with a stick.

"Where did I get this number? Well—"

More growling.

"Yeah, I know you're a thousand miles away. But we were hoping—"

I reached out my hand. "Stephen, give me the phone."

"Former Agent Gallagher? I'm Carolyn Neville, Stephen's supervisor. I'll go straight to the point. Would you like the chance to bring down the Boudreauxs?"

"Lady, for all I know *you* work for them." His voice was gruff and not in an endearing Wilford Brimley way.

"From what I've heard, the family is way too smart to use a ridiculous story like ours to scam you. They're not desperate, but we are."

"Who'd you say you work for?"

"Pendleton House Publishers."

"Give me a minute. I'll call you back."

The line went dead.

"What did he say?" Stuart asked.

"I think he's checking us out."

Five minutes later, we'd moved a good 300 feet down the highway. I looked for an exit to anywhere, but we were firmly implanted.

My ringtone sounded.

"All right," Gallagher said. "I'm in Chicago. You're in New York. Let's meet halfway."

"Where would that be?"

"Ever been to Columbus, Ohio?"

"Can't say I have."

"Me neither. Let's hope the family doesn't think of looking for us there."

"It's going to take us a while."

"I don't doubt it. Check in with me on the way. And keep your head down."

"Thank you," I said.

"Don't speak too soon. At least one of us is going to regret this."

A click, then silence.

"So, what'd he say?" Stephen asked.

"He's in. At least for the moment." I paused. "Ever been to Columbus, Ohio?"

"No."

"If we're lucky, we'll be there in two days. If not, we'll be history."

CHAPTER 4

"I NEED MY STUFF," STEPHEN WHINED AS WE FINALLY LEFT Manhattan. "What am I supposed to wear? And my guitar—"

"You don't need one," I said.

"We can't go home and pack our bags," Stuart said, looking like he wished we could. "Jeremy, or whoever's following us, will look there first."

"We need less fragrant wardrobes anyway," I said. Seeing a red-and-white Target sign in the distance, I took the exit to East River Plaza.

Stephen and Stuart headed for the men's clothing department. I lingered long enough to hear them arguing about whether Walmart would have been a classier choice.

I'd been wanting something breezier for summer, which really meant something looser so I could meet my donut quota. I envisioned something pink—the more inappropriate for the office the better.

One set of underwear might be enough, but of course you can't buy bras and panties at Target that way. My choices were basic, sturdy, gray, the kind of thing one might expect editors to wear.

The jeans and blouses were pretty picked over, mostly not my size, and the only pink things were the markdown tags. Not wanting to take time to try anything on, I did the best I could and eyeballed each candidate. I ended up with a light green blouse, a pair of jeans, and a denim jacket with a reddish-brown spot I managed to pick off with my fingernails.

"We're done," said a voice behind me. It was Stephen, holding up an Ed Sheeran T-shirt, black jeans, and two three-packs of white socks and briefs. Stuart had rolled his choices into a big wad, apparently for reasons of secrecy or embarrassment.

Stephen, Mr. Impulse Buy, grabbed a bag of Werther's caramels at the checkout. Stuart got a little plastic vial of Tylenol.

Thanking God for credit cards, I led the way back to the car. We stopped at a Shell station and changed in the bathroom. Not wanting to set off the fire alarm, I resisted the urge to incinerate my old garments in the 50-gallon drum that served as a trash can.

We met in the convenience store and purchased drinks. I got a Coke the size of a roll of paper towels, just for the caffeine.

"I'll drive," Stephen said as I filled the tank with regular unleaded.

I shook my head. "Not that I don't trust you with my car. But I don't."

I drove and drove, trying not to listen to the basketball game Stephen was streaming on his phone. Stuart, dressed in what turned out to be a cleaner version of practically everything he was already wearing, slept fitfully. Every so often he'd awake with a start, look out the window, and pop a Tylenol.

"You'll damage your liver if you keep that up," I warned.

"I was hoping for something more serious," he muttered, and curled up in the fetal position—or at least as much as one could manage with a seat belt on.

The sun was setting as we hit Lancaster County, Pennsylvania. I was out of Coke, jittery as a chihuahua, glancing at red barns with hexes like stained glass and wondering where we were going to stay. Stephen pulled out his phone and, as usual, was compelled to enlighten us.

"That's for good luck," he said, pointing at one. "The next one's for fertility."

"I need the first one tattooed on my arm," I said.

"Insert your own joke about the other," he said, trying to look innocent.

"I'd rather not." I took the last swig of Coke and stowed the bottle under the passenger seat.

"Did you see *Witness?* The movie with Harrison Ford?"

I nodded. "Didn't everybody?"

"He stayed in a barn like these."

"Don't think so. That took place in Amish country. This is Pennsylvania Dutch. The Amish are religious but the P.D.s are ethnic. German, to be specific."

He was silent, probably pouting.

"That's my best impression of you," I said.

"Very funny."

It was getting dark when I noticed a sign down the road. QUILTER'S REST, it said. I turned into the small and half-empty parking lot. The place was unbearably quaint, trimmed with a half-mile of white bric-a-brac, the office window framing an unlit kerosene lantern.

A plump woman in a light blue dress, white bonnet, and yellow apron checked us in. A cigarette butt with a tendril of smoke rising from it lay in an ashtray on the counter.

"Any place to eat around here?" I asked wearily, filling out a form and having trouble remembering my license plate number.

She pointed down the road. "Just past the feed store. Pretty much your only choice. Windmill Cafe."

After dumping our stuff in the two rooms we'd been assigned, we followed her directions.

The restaurant's lot was sparsely populated, too. "No buggies?" Stephen asked.

"Quit thinking Amish," I said.

An unexpectedly skinny girl in an all-denim outfit handed us menus. "We're out of everything except sausage, sauerkraut, and pie."

"Okay," I said. "I'll have one of everything."

"So will I," Stephen said.

Stuart sighed. "I'll be sorry, but me, too."

The sausage was greasy, the sauerkraut sauer, the pie was a tart lemon meringue. My gorge was rising as we split the bill and left a tip.

Back at the Quilter's Rest, Stephen and Stuart were stuck together. I got my own room.

Between indigestion and worrying about who might find us, I had a hard time sleeping. About midnight I heard a crash from next door. Rising from bed, still clad in my green blouse and jeans, I grabbed my pepper spray from my purse and ventured into the hallway.

Stephen answered my knock. "Stuart bumped into the desk on his fourth trip to the bathroom. And he's so nervous about Jeremy that it just makes it worse. How about you trade places with me?" He rubbed his bloodshot eyes.

"If I were Amish and this was *Rumspringa*, it might be proper. But I'm not and it isn't."

"What the heck is *Rumspringa*?"

I started to answer, but Stuart's groans were too pathetic.

I handed him my pepper spray. "You need this more than I do," I said.

* * *

Next morning we met in the hallway to compare sleep-deprivation stories. The circles under our eyes were the color of coffee, a cup of which we held in our shaky grips.

"Oh, what a night," I mumbled.

"The Four Seasons," Stephen said. "Late December, back in '63 . . ."

Stuart took a sip. "Sorry about last night," he said, looking down at the brown carpet I imagined harbored a multitude of silverfish. "Must have lost about ten pounds. Maybe I should do a diet book."

"Anybody up for breakfast?" I asked, hoping nobody would say yes. Nobody did.

We didn't have the strength to *hit* the road, exactly, so we just drove on it. Or I did, doing my best not to drift off.

"No white Cadillacs yet," Stuart said, tapping a Tylenol out of his vial and discovering it was empty.

"Did you see *Christine?*" Stephen asked.

"Christine who?" Stuart groused, trying to lick the inside of the tube.

"Stephen King movie about a possessed car."

"You mean *re*possessed?"

"*Demon*-possessed. Stuart, you've got to keep up with pop culture if you're going to relate to your audience."

I snorted. "*Christine* came out in the late eighties."

Stephen frowned. "Maybe I meant the remake in 2016. Certified Fresh on Rotten Tomatoes."

"I never saw either one," Stuart said, sinking lower in his seat.

"Okay, how about *Duel?* Directed by Spielberg. Very

different. About a possessed *semi-truck*. Starred Dennis Weaver. Released in 1971."

"That's even older," I said.

"You know Dennis Weaver, right? Chester on *Gunsmoke?*"

"You're getting positively prehistoric," I said.

"*Gunsmoke* I've heard of," mumbled Stuart. "*Duel* I wouldn't know from *Hamilton.*"

Stephen leaned forward as if to share a secret. "Weaver was probably more famous for playing Marshal Matt Dillon's sidekick, Chester. He was replaced by Ken Curtis as Festus. Not many people know why."

He paused, waiting for us to beg for details. We ignored him.

"Weaver got a swelled head and wanted to move on to better things. He went on to play McCloud, a sheriff with one of those wooly-collared jackets. Whether that was better is a matter of—"

"Uh-oh," Stuart said, looking out the back window.

I checked the mirror. The road was straight enough that I could see what appeared to be a white Cadillac a mile or so behind us.

"Time to take a back road," I said.

"I thought this *was* a back road," Stephen said.

We passed more barns and hexes, but no alternate routes. Finally an old sign saying SMUCKER'S WAY appeared on the right, and I took it. Still paved, but potholed.

There being no speed limit sign, I accelerated to about 40. But rounding a corner I suddenly came upon a pair of Amish-looking black buggies with red triangular signs on their rears. Stomping the brake, which protested with the screech of a night owl, I stopped just short of hitting the one directly ahead.

"Thought you said we weren't in Amish country yet," Stephen said.

"I was misinformed."

We crawled along for a mile or so. Couldn't pass.

Stuart cleared his throat. "I can't tell anymore whether my ideas are good, but I have one." He paused. "Maybe we should buy some Amish clothes and hide out in a barn like Harrison Ford did in *Witness*."

There was silence, except for the *clip-clop* of the horses in front of us.

"Nothing personal, but that's a crazy idea," Stephen said.

I frowned. "You should talk."

I looked in the rearview mirror. "Very creative, Stuart. But we won't be safe until we get to Mr. Gallagher in Columbus."

"If then," Stuart said with a sigh.

More *clip-clop*.

"Let's think positive," I said brightly, and smiled.

As I always said, it was best to say the opposite of what you were thinking.

* * *

Against my better judgment, I surrendered the wheel a few miles later. Letting anyone else drive my car was anathema to me, but given our lack of velocity the risk seemed small.

We took turns maneuvering the back roads for several hours, watching the woods go by. At one point Stephen, who was driving, started listing the varieties of foliage he observed. I punched the radio button and turned up the volume on NPR's *Car Talk*. He got the message but said nothing.

Despite the deepening darkness, I couldn't nap. I was determined to monitor the vigilance of my colleagues. Stuart seemed to squint a lot. "My night vision stinks," he said offhandedly.

I made a show of checking my watch. "Oh, look. Your shift is over."

"But—"

"You'll thank me later."

Finally we came to a major highway. The lights of Columbus glowed in the distance.

Stephen stretched in the back seat. "Thought we'd never get to civilization again. Or get my appetite back."

I turned to Stuart. "How's your stomach?"

"Better than my head."

The first Columbus exit came none too soon. I stopped at the first familiar-looking motel, a Rodeway Inn. We got two rooms and freshened up, which in my case meant washing my face and using half my stick of deodorant.

We'd spotted a Subway down the street, and I appointed myself to pick up a few sandwiches. After taking orders, I walked the well-lit sidewalk, searching for white Cadillacs. Same thing on the way back. Nothing more threatening than an oversized red pickup full of guys wearing baseball caps, wolf-whistling and yelling what they apparently felt were compliments on my appearance. I pretended to be offended.

We congregated in my room, where I passed out the submarines, chips, and drinks. Stephen had asked for a chocolate-chip cookie, which I conveniently forgot.

"I can't keep paying for everything," I said, sitting on the edge of the bed. "When all this is over, we split the bills equally. And don't think I won't keep track."

After asking an open-eyed blessing, I bit into my Cold Cut Combo and started chewing. Stephen attacked his meat-ball sandwich, a mess of barbecue sauce and shreds of lettuce that dropped to the carpet. Stuart, who'd chosen a tuna salad, was more dainty.

"Maybe we should call Mr. Gallagher," he said.

I shook my head. "Too late."

He shrugged. "I suppose you're right."

We finished our repast. I handed Stephen a tan-and-green napkin and pointed at the blobs of lettuce and mayo. "Cleanliness may not be next to godliness, but this is my room."

With a grunt he licked his fingers and went to work. I bade them farewell and dropped the cups and wrappers in the wastebasket.

I watched about 15 minutes of the local news, then fell into bed. I'd almost drifted off when my phone jangled on the nightstand.

"Ms. Neville?" It was Gallagher, his voice raspy. "Sorry to call so late. Trying to quit smoking, and nicotine withdrawal's keeping me up."

"We may have seen Jeremy's Cadillac this morning."

"Catch a license number?"

"Too far away."

He sighed. "I assume you're staying in a motel in Columbus."

"Right."

"I'd recommend moving your car out of sight if you haven't already."

"Whatever you say."

"Now here's the deal. Let's meet in the morning at the Columbus Zoo and Aquarium. I'm sure you can get directions."

"What time?"

"Oh, say nine o'clock. Get an Uber or a taxi to throw Jeremy off the trail if he's around."

"Okay."

"Never been to the zoo, but I see on the Internet they've got a Reptile House. We'll meet there."

"I hate snakes."

"You'd hate meeting up with Jeremy a lot more. I'll be the

bald guy in the tan raincoat pacing back and forth and trying not to think about having a cigarette."

He hung up.

I got dressed and moved the car under a tree in the back, then threw every possible lock and latch on my room.

After jamming two chairs against the door, I switched off the light, prayed, and fell asleep.

CHAPTER 5

NEXT MORNING, ABOUT TEN, WE TOOK AN UBER TO THE ZOO.
The driver, a gray-haired lady with a British accent, took us
down West Powell Road and dropped us at the entrance.

"Give me a call when you're done," she said. "And give my
regards to the Komodo Dragon."

There was already a line at the entrance under the leop-
ard-skin banner that said ZOO and ZOOMBEZI BAY,
mostly moms with preschoolers. "Who's paying?" Stephen
asked.

"Your turn," I said. "I got the Uber."

Ahead of us was a little girl in a yellow dress, maybe four
years old, begging her mother for an elephant-shaped
balloon. When Mom resisted, she stopped her entreaties long
enough to throw up. I guess some people can do that on
command. I'm that way with cracking my knuckles, but only
use it in emergencies.

After squeezing through the turnstile, I waited in front of
the Salty Seal Gift Shop while Stuart took considerably more
time and effort in accomplishing the same. Searching the
crowd, I saw no one resembling anybody I didn't want to see.

I examined the map in my hand. "Let's skip the aquarium."

Stuart, trembling slightly as usual, seemed disappointed. "But I love the electric eels. Always been fascinated by them. Did you know they're related to catfish? And they have to surface every ten minutes to breathe. They can deliver a shock of 650 volts. And—"

"You're starting to sound like Stephen. Maybe you've spent a little too much time around those repulsive things already."

I folded up my map. "Maybe we can come back when we're done with Mr. Gallagher."

He looked around and bit his lip. "We're too exposed here."

"Don't worry," I said. "This is the last place Jeremy will look. And the Reptile House is even more private."

Following the signs, we found ourselves facing an older, low-slung building with lots of stone. Inside it was humid, smelling of sweat but not much else.

To no one's surprise, Stephen took out his phone and began to enlighten us about our scaly friends and enemies. "That brown one on the fake rock's a reticulated python. Over there's an eyelash viper, the little yellow one peeking through the leaves." Neither animal even twitched, perhaps lulled to docility by his lecture.

"Next we have the spider tortoise. He often lives to the ripe old age of—"

"Oh, look," Stuart mercifully interrupted. "The Komodo Dragon. Almost as interesting as the electric eel." He pointed at a Doberman-sized creature with scaly green skin, the spitting image of a bogus dinosaur from a really bad science-fiction movie.

"World's largest living lizard," he continued. Flicking its forked tongue, the thing slid into a swamp-deep water tank.

Stuart took out his phone, pressed a button, and started recording. "Note to self: Work Komodo Dragon into next Jennifer story." He turned it off. "If I survive," he mumbled.

My armpits were starting to tingle. "I think I'll stop by the girls' room," I said. "My Ophidiophobia's kicking in."

Stephen poked his phone again.

"Let me save you some time," I said. "It means fear of snakes."

"I know that," he said loftily. "Just wanted to confirm."

The restroom was clean but steamy, apparently unoccupied. There being no other place to take refuge, I sat on a toilet and locked the stall door.

Women and children came and went for several minutes. I started to nod off.

Suddenly there was a knock two feet from my face. "Carolyn Neville?" a woman asked.

I froze. "Who wants to know?"

"Some guy asked me to get you."

"What does he look like? About thirty, messed-up hair, oily?"

"Uh . . . no. More like an old bald guy in a tan raincoat."

I breathed a sigh of relief. "I'll be right there."

I heard the door close behind her. By now I actually had to use the facilities, the details of which are unnecessary to recount.

As soon as I flushed, the knocking resumed. "You in there?" growled the former agent. "Jeez, you women take forever in the can."

I opened the door. "Don't you need a search warrant or something?"

"Not under the circumstances."

I went to the sink and washed up. "I can see we're going to get along famously."

"Hey, we don't have all day. Let's find ourselves a dark little corner where we can all talk."

A woman came in, towing a toddler. When she saw Gallagher, she gasped.

"Sorry," he muttered.

Smirking, I followed him out.

* * *

I hadn't noticed it before, but Agent Gallagher had a large manila envelope under his arm. He made a circle-the-wagons gesture to get us rounded up. The sounds of children running and parents berating echoed in the mostly-stone chamber.

He raised two fingers to his lips as if preparing to smoke an absent cigarette, then saved face by scratching the side of his nose.

"In case you're wondering why they say I'm obsessed with the Boudreaux family, here're some things you should know. First, back in 1967 a guy in Boston named Pete had a problem with betting on the horses. His glasses were rose-colored, and his instincts were terrible.

"He hid it from his wife and kids as long as he could, especially the part about borrowing big-time cash from an up-and-coming loan shark named Max Boudreaux. Started drinking. Max didn't have much of a staff in those days, so he followed Pete home from a bar one night, blocked his way with a light blue Chevy Impala, and pulled out a gun."

I looked around to see whether a crowd was gathering to hear his story. So far, the snakes were more interesting.

"Pete was 42," Gallagher continued. "If you saw him you'd swear he was ten years older. Between the debt and the booze, he couldn't hold up to the stress. Max never had to use his gun. Next morning cops found Pete dead, propped up next to a tree. Heart attack."

He paused, and I could imagine him taking a long draw on that imaginary cigarette and slowly exhaling. "Pete was my dad."

We looked at each other. Stephen proved he didn't know what to say by shaking his head and offering the former agent a stick of Dentyne. Maybe because his mouth needed something to do, Gallagher accepted.

"I've been lugging this rogue's gallery around for at least fifteen years," he said, pulling out a blurry photocopy and holding up a picture of an older man with thinning gray hair and thick glasses. Lots of liver spots on his face. He was smiling, showing off a set of unnaturally white dentures. "This is Max. Always thought he looked a little like that actor, James Garner. But don't let the smile fool you."

He took out another. "His daughter, Angel." Fortyish, angular, blonde. "Never smiles except when she's around her father or has killed an addict who couldn't pay."

Stuart shivered.

"Looks like Jane Lynch," Stephen said.

"Who?" Gallagher asked.

"Never mind."

Next was Jeremy. "We've met," I said.

One more photo. "Even the Bureau doesn't know her name," the former agent said. "New hire. Being trained on the job."

He handed me the picture. Early twenties, lean. Short, strawberry blonde hair. Leather jacket. Could have been my daughter, but thank God she wasn't.

"Let's call her the Nameless Girl," Stephen said.

"Why?"

"Sounds creepy."

Gallagher rolled his eyes. "The Boudreauxs are based in

the Big Easy, but they're really everywhere. You name it, they're into it—loans, yeah, but they make a heck of a lot more in drugs and prostitution."

He turned to Stuart. "You're the victim, right?"

Stuart nodded sheepishly.

"Don't tell me. You lost so much at the tables you couldn't get out. Now you're in hock to these animals and aren't safe anywhere."

Gallagher shoved the portraits back in the envelope. "And now these innocent bystanders don't have anywhere to go, either." He nodded toward us.

"I didn't mean for it to turn out that way," Stuart said faintly.

"What in blazes is the matter with you?"

Instead of responding, Stuart nervously cast an eye about for anyone who might match the pictures we'd just seen. "God knows I didn't want to get them involved."

Gallagher said something a lot worse than *blazes*. "Come over here," he added, leading the way out of the corner and into the snake department.

He pointed at a small red-and-black reptile. "Coral snake. Second-strongest venom in the world. Get bit by this bad boy, you're dead in twelve hours or less."

Stephen was poking his phone. "Actually, you're much worse off with a king cobra. Deadliest anywhere."

Gallagher grunted. "So what? My point is these little devils are nothing compared to the Boudreauxs."

"Point taken," I said.

He scratched his chin. "My former employer won't jump into the snake pit. Guess I don't blame 'em. Most agents have families. Thanks to the Boudreauxs, I don't. Nothing to lose. I'll risk everything to bring 'em down."

He made the fingers-to-lips gesture again.

"I won't lie to you. Since you've gotten in the family's way, you'll all have to do the same."

Not surprising, but I swallowed anyway.

"God, I need a smoke," he said.

I wanted to give him one, but patted him on the shoulder instead.

* * *

Stuart still stared at the coral snake. I half expected him to stick his hand in the terrarium and get it all over with.

"What's your plan?" I asked Gallagher, who was tapping his envelope on the wall with nervous energy.

He looked over my shoulder. "The family won't stop until they either get the money or get rid of all of us. How much cash could the three of you raise?"

I called Stephen and Stuart over; he repeated the question.

"Kind of personal, isn't it?" Stephen asked.

Gallagher scoffed. "So is being on the receiving end of a power drill."

"Wow," Stephen said. "What do they do with it?"

"You don't want to know."

Stuart raised a hand. "I've got about thirty thousand in the bank."

"I can spare ten," I said.

"Ten *dollars?*" Stephen cried.

"*Thousand,*" I said. "Not that I can actually *spare* it. I am, after all, an editor."

"I'm in for five thousand," Gallagher said. "Federal pensions aren't all they're cracked up to be."

Stephen shook his head. "If I sell my guitar, I might get six hundred. It's a Fender Stratocaster. Signed by—"

"No time to go on eBay, kid," Gallagher said.

"Two hundred then. My rent's impossible."

I did some quick arithmetic in my head. "Not nearly enough."

"Then you need a place to go until we can get a mole into the mansion," the former agent said.

"How about the witness protection program?" I asked.

He shook his head. "You're not testifying against the Boudreauxs. You just need a safe place to stay."

While we all pondered that, a sudden loud POP sounded behind us. I almost lost my balance on the slimy floor. Stuart gasped. Stephen dropped his smartphone, which landed with a *crack*. Whirling, Gallagher slipped a hand under his coat. I hadn't thought about whether he'd have a gun.

There stood a mom and a wailing preschooler. A blob of brown rubber on a string dangled from his fist. Judging from the more intact wares of a nearby balloon vendor, it had been a snake only moments before.

Gallagher stood down, looking like he wanted to spit. Stuart rubbed his forehead with the heel of his palm. Stephen, swearing, picked up his phone and poked to make sure it still worked.

"Any darker corners around here?" I asked. "And quieter?"

Stuart looked at his map. "The aquarium, maybe."

We worked our way back there. I wanted to play chameleon and dart from palm tree to palm tree, camouflaged. Had to settle for slinking like a salamander and holding my map to the side of my face.

I'd hoped for one of those huge, glassed-in hallways where sharks and whales wheel in circles under, over, and beside you. But all the big sea life was in outdoor pools. We ended up in the 4D Theater, huddling in the back row and waiting for the lights to go down.

The place wasn't packed. "I need popcorn," Stephen said.

"Nothing personal," I whispered, "but please sit down and shut up."

He plopped into his seat and folded his arms. "Just for that, I won't tell you my idea."

"Our loss," I said.

"Go ahead," Gallagher mumbled.

"We could stay with the Amish."

Long pause.

"So riding in the car behind a couple of buggies makes you an expert on the Amish?" I asked.

"No. But *Witness* proved it can be done."

"That was *fiction*," Stuart whispered.

Gallagher looked at the ceiling. "Not the craziest thing I've ever hear, but it's close."

I shook my head. "How's it supposed to work? Why in the world would they take us in?"

Stephen leaned forward. "They're *kind*, right? Forgiving and all that?"

"Yes, but—"

"And you're religious. You could talk them into it."

I tried to think of an intelligent response, but could only manage a sputter.

Stuart looked thoughtful. "It's the craziest idea *I've* ever heard. But I don't have another one. And I'm in no position to argue."

The lights were going down. "The only way to stop the Boudreauxs," Gallagher said, "is to use you three as bait and nab them before they pull the trigger. Or whatever Jeremy did to the guy at the golf course."

I settled back in my seat and closed my eyes. It made a lot of sense if you were Harrison Ford. I wasn't even Emily Blunt.

"But you'll have to find a way to do it without endangering the Amish," Gallagher advised. "Crap like kindness and forgiveness don't mean a thing to Max. Or Angel."

The movie started. The music came up. I stared at the toothy sharks and toothier dolphin trainers, counting my blessings and coming up with zero.

Gallagher touched my shoulder. "Talk to you soon," he said, and left.

It was the only way, I guessed. Except for all the others, like suicide and plastic surgery.

"Can I get my popcorn now?" Stephen whispered.

"Only if you pick me up a tub of Milk Duds."

"They don't come in a tub."

"Then make it two boxes, the longest Twizzler you can find, and a thirty-two-ounce cup of anything wet."

It might not be my last meal but if things turned out the way I feared, there'd be no time to choose the menu.

CHAPTER 6

THE TRUTH WAS I KNEW PRACTICALLY NOTHING ABOUT THE Amish except what I'd read. *Rumspringa*, suspenders, straw hats, shoofly pie—that was about it, except for their trademark peacemaking.

The closest I'd gotten to an Amish guy was a Mennonite sophomore named Sam I'd dated in college. He dressed in Levis, never wore a hat, and was surprisingly carnal-minded. After two weeks of fighting him off on the dorm lounge's couch, I gave him his walking papers.

I didn't mention that, of course, on the way back to the motel.

"Better start practicing our Amishness," Stephen said, prodding his phone.

"Okay," I said. "I forgive you for being such a jerk."

He ignored me. "Maybe I should grow a beard."

Stuart groaned. "Do we have to? If I don't shave every day, I start itching."

"Harrison Ford didn't grow one," I said.

He breathed a sigh of relief.

"Do they say stuff like *thee* and *thou?*" Stephen asked. "'Cause I don't think I can do that and sound natural."

"Look it up," I said.

There was silence from the back seat. Finally he gave a grunt and leaned forward. "No *thees* and *thous*. At least not enough to shake a dowsing stick at. Some of them have a weird accent where they say *mischeef* instead of *mischief*."

"Doubt we'll be using that word on a daily basis," I said. "Same with *handkercheef* and *sneef*."

Pulling into the motel parking lot, I suggested we meet later for dinner at the Burger King next to the Subway. "I'm going to consult with one of the world's greatest authorities on the plain people."

"Who?" Stephen asked.

"My mother."

He started to ask something else, like what made her such an expert, but probably figured he'd antagonized me enough for one day.

In my room I got out my phone and prepared to hit speed dial. Then I paused in midair.

I loved Betty Neville, but sometimes there seemed to be something between us—something as thick as Hoover Dam and high as one of those super-skyscrapers in Qatar and the United Arab Emirates that made the Sears Tower look like a car wash.

We talked every couple of weeks, my dad on the extension and saying *huh* every few minutes. Almost always we finished with a brief interrogation about my love life. Dad knew better than to bring that up, but Mom couldn't seem to resist. I'd learned to keep things as vague as possible, usually mentioning some guy I'd seen on the street, describing him and saying he was a possibility if only I could find the time. Then came the sighs and the *I-love-yous* and Dad's sleepy-sounding *me-toos*.

Resolving to keep things noncontroversial this time, I pushed the button and connected with Idaho Falls. Mom answered, breathless as usual. She was healthy, but a little too fond of her own cooking.

"Carolyn, sweetheart, I was just making lunch. Vegetable soup. No celery this time. Your dad hates it."

"Oh. Well, I can call back."

"No, no. I'm just starting it now. Your father's not here, though."

"That's fine. I mainly need to talk to *you*."

She made a concerned noise. "What's wrong, dear?"

"You're a big fan of Christian novels, right? Especially the Amish ones."

"Oh, my word, yes. Wanda Brunstetter, Kathryn Cushman, Cindy Woodsmall, and especially Beverly Lewis."

"I've got some questions."

She sounded excited. "Carolyn, are you finally going to work for a godly publisher? Not that you have to, but you know how I feel about—"

"I do. And no, I'm still working for Pendleton House."

"I see." I could hear the disappointment, but it wasn't the first time. "Fire away," she said.

"Umm . . . are most of them farmers?"

"Yes. But they make furniture, too, and some wonderful food. And they have roofing companies. I've seen ads in the newspaper for some kind of electric Amish fireplace, but that doesn't sound right, does it? The pictures look so fake, like a bunch of cab drivers with pasted-on beards."

I had a pad of paper and pen on the nightstand, but they didn't seem necessary yet. "Are there different kinds of Amish, like Baptists and Methodists?"

"They're either Old Order or New Order."

I started writing. "How do they feel about the rest of us?"

"They call us *the world* or *the English*. They don't seem to mind us, but I'm sure they think we're misinformed."

"If I were Amish, what would I do in a typical day?"

"Weekday or Sunday?"

"Weekday."

"Depends on how old you are. You'd probably get up before dawn, milk the cows or start making breakfast. People have different assignments. The men go to the fields, or their businesses; the women tend to the chores and raising the children. Oh, and some of the men work in factories. A lot of them take naps after lunch."

"Uh-huh."

"I read one book where an Amish woman about your age wanted to be more like the men. She used a saw to cut some poles for a barn raising and cut off three toes. She wrapped her foot in a towel and—"

"I get the picture."

"Of course, her husband disapproved. But he came to understand that she needed to be herself, to use the gifts the Lord gave her. Just one reason to find a good man and settle down."

I sighed. "Right."

"Hey, you know what? You should go to this website, amishamerica.com. You probably don't have time to read all of Beverly Lewis' books." She paused. "How come you need to know all this, honey?"

"I'll . . . be visiting an Amish community soon."

"Oh, it's about time you took a vacation. Send us some pictures, will you?"

"I'll do my best."

"Anything else? Are you eating right? Any nice men on the horizon?"

"I'm fine, Mom."

"Whoops. My soup's boiling over. I'll tell Dad you called."

"Love you," I said.

"Me, too."

I didn't have time to fact-check her info, but most of it sounded believable.

Like I said, I love her to death.

But, as always, I was reminded why we don't talk more often.

* * *

Next morning it took six hours to get back to Pennsylvania. When I saw my first hex barn, I slowed down.

"I'm hungry," Stephen said.

"One thing at a time," I said. "First we need directions to a community that'll take us in. Then we need clothes."

A sign that said GENUINE AMISH FURNITURE loomed down the road. "Must be fake," Stephen said. "Like 'genuine' cubic zirconium."

"Whatever." I set the turn signal. "Not looking for trundle beds today anyway."

There were rocking chairs all over the porch. I expected a dog, or at least a chicken, to be dozing next to a pickle barrel. All I saw was what looked like a dead frog under the threshold.

A little bell over the screen door tinkled as we entered. The showroom was the size of a one-room schoolhouse, paneled with knotty pine and smelling of sawdust.

A bearded man wearing a leather apron looked up from the counter and nodded. "Afternoon," he said. No salesman's sparkly smile, just honest eyes and a jaw like Abraham Lincoln's. I liked Amish life already.

"Is there anything you're especially looking for?" he asked.

"Actually, yes. But it's not a piece of furniture."

"Oh. We have refreshments if you like."

Stephen looked around eagerly.

"Later," I said.

A middle-aged woman in gray dress and white bonnet emerged from a back room, looking like she'd just sucked a whole basketful of lemons. "Can I help you?"

"They're not looking for furniture," the clerk said.

She raised her chin and narrowed her eyes. "If you've come to steal our recipes or take pictures of us with your 'smartphones,' I must ask you to leave."

Stephen leaned toward me. "They believe having your picture taken steals your soul."

The woman looked tired, as if she'd had this conversation too many times. "You are thinking of some Native Americans. For us, it is a matter of making a graven image. Many of our young ones don't agree. They take pictures of themselves in front of their lunches and send them to others who apparently have nothing to do."

"No pictures," I said. "No recipes, either. Just an unusual question."

She waited, one gray eyebrow raised.

"We're interested in taking a . . . *retreat* by living in one of your communities for a short time."

She looked at the clerk. He shrugged.

"I've never heard of such a thing," she said.

"Did you see *Witness?*" Stephen asked.

"The movie?"

"Yes."

"Of course not. A few of the others have. I pray for them."

She turned on her heel and walked into the back. The clerk looked at the floor, shaking his head.

The woman was back in a minute or so, followed by a shy-looking man in his thirties. He was beardless, red-faced, still holding a wooden mallet in his hand. He reminded me of that actor, John Krasinski, but more square-jawed.

"This is my son, Aaron," the woman announced. I couldn't tell whether she was bragging or apologizing, since everything she said came out like a police summons.

She repeated what we'd said, then waited. He looked as baffled as the other two had.

"You'll have to speak to Bishop Stoltzfus," he said. "His place is about five miles from here on Smoker Road. Turn right, then left."

Stephen stepped up. "Know where we can get some Amish clothes?"

Aaron started to say something, but the woman interrupted. "Deal with the inner man before the outer one."

"Fine by me," Stephen said, and examined the snack rack at the register. "Hey, Cashew Crunch! I'll take two bags."

Stuart ambled over. "Beefstick for me."

The clerk rang them up.

The woman shook her head. "Snacks. Aaron's idea."

"Thank you," I said. "You've been very helpful."

Her expression said she regretted it.

I looked at Aaron. He looked at me, then away, blushing.

My face felt awfully warm.

"Perhaps we'll see you again," I said.

"If the Lord wills."

I hoped He did.

* * *

Next day, bright and early, we pulled up at the Stoltzfus farm. The barn was red as a raw steak, the house white clapboard with a welcoming porch. A windmill sat about 50 feet away.

"Nice place," Stephen said.

"Pure Norman Rockwell," Stuart added, but still seemed nervous.

A mid-sixtyish woman in traditional clothes and wire-rimmed glasses answered our knock. She reminded me of Nurse Ratched at the furniture store, only with more honey than vinegar. A little girl, a miniature version of her in every way, peeked around the door frame.

"Yes?" the woman asked.

I made the usual introductions, invoking Aaron's name to gain credibility. She looked puzzled, a bit worried. "Just a moment," she said, and closed the door.

We looked at each other. "We're screwed," Stuart said. "And I can't say I blame her."

Soon she was back. "Come in," she said.

"This is my husband, Bishop Stoltzfus." A gray-haired man, at least 70, sat in a well-worn overstuffed chair. He put down a magazine with a tractor on the cover and took off his reading glasses. Rising to his feet, he extended a hand. As he shook I could feel the calluses.

"Welcome," he said, not quite smiling. There was a gentleness about him that softened the impression he made, kind of like a cross between a pilgrim and an undertaker.

"Forgive me if we seem inhospitable," he said. "We don't get many strangers here."

"The people at the furniture store seemed to respect your authority," I said. "I can see why."

He chuckled. "For us, a bishop is a servant. I am a volunteer and oversee two districts." He paused and looked from me to Stephen to Stuart. "Let's sit down, shall we?"

As we settled his wife entered, trailed by her Mini-Me. "Would you care for garden tea or lemonade?"

We all picked lemonade. The little girl—her granddaughter, I assumed—went to work on a wooden jigsaw puzzle by the Genuine Amish Fireplace.

"Are you Old Order or New Order?" I asked as Mrs. Stoltzfus handed me a Mason jar of lemonade.

"New," the Bishop said. "But we have no issue with our more traditional brethren." A hint of a smile curled above his beard. "Why, I've even broken bread with a Baptist."

"I'm practically one of those." I paused. "We have a request. It's more than a bit out of the ordinary."

"I see," he said, and sipped his drink.

I explained our situation. Stephen kept interrupting to mansplain. I failed to show the proper gratitude.

When I was done the Bishop shook his head. "Sounds like *Witness*."

"You've *seen* that?" Stuart exclaimed.

"Thankfully, no. Our daughter told us about it before she left."

The smile left his face; his faded blue eyes were pools of sadness. There was a story there, but I didn't want to know it.

"The last thing I'd want to do is endanger the community," I said.

The Bishop and his wife gazed at each other. I wondered how long they'd been married. Each seemed to know what the other was thinking.

"Hebrews 13:12," he said. "Show hospitality to strangers. We may be entertaining angels without knowing it."

She looked away.

He bowed his head and closed his eyes, apparently praying.

The silence was long. I looked over at Stephen, who was fidgeting in his Genuine Amish Chair. It may have been awkward for Stephen and Stuart, but holy for me.

The Bishop raised his head. "There is a smaller barn at the edge of our property. Would you be willing to stay there?"

"It was good enough for Harrison Ford," Stephen said.

"Would you wear plain clothes and work beside us?"

I nodded.

"You must stay no longer than two weeks. And one more thing: Please report daily to Aaron, the young deacon who works at the furniture shop."

Stephen looked at me and grinned mis*chee*viously.

I ignored him.

"It's a deal," I said, trying not to look too happy.

CHAPTER 7

BEING UNREADY TO PLAY PLAINPEOPLE, WE WENT TO A MOTEL. I expected to see a sign that at least silhouetted a horse and buggy, maybe named SCRAPPLE INN AND SUITES, but it only said LODGING.

We checked in. The man behind the desk looked like Methuselah's grandfather. He was dressed in a gray Philadelphia Eagles sweatshirt. I had to guess the rest, the counter standing in the way.

Apparently hard of hearing, he cupped his hand to his hairy, long-lobed ear as I asked whether we could get a couple of rooms.

"Say again?"

I turned up the volume. "We'd like to stay."

He grinned. His teeth were so few and far between I could have counted them at a glance if I'd had the stomach for it.

"Sign here," he said, pushing a dusty ledger in my direction. I looked around for the quill pen, but found only a ballpoint that said LANCASTER COUNTY BANK on it.

To my surprise, he took a credit card. But this time it was Stephen's.

"Not fair," he said. "I'm just a poor boy; I need some sympathy . . ."

I snorted. "Don't misquote 'Bohemian Rhapsody.' That's heresy. You'll get no sympathy from me."

The ancient desk clerk held out two key cards. "Rooms 211 and 212."

"Thanks."

"If you want anything, give me a ring. But I'm dead to the world after nine p.m." He turned and walked back behind a curtain, allowing me to confirm that he was indeed dressed from the waist down.

"Let's go to my room," I said, and handed Stuart the key to 212. "Want to call Mr. Gallagher."

The decor in 211 was early yard sale, and not the kind of stuff you'd want to buy. But the smell of Febreze was reassuring. Sitting on the bed, I took out my phone and hit SPEAKER.

When I got Gallagher's voice mail, I sighed. At the beep I said, "Mr. Gallagher, if you're there, pick up. It's Carolyn Neville."

There was a click. "Where are you?"

"Lancaster County. An Amish community's agreed to take us in for two weeks. God knows why. We're at a motel now."

"Is your car out of sight?"

"Yeah, I think so."

There was a snapping sound.

"I'm hearing a weird noise."

"Nicotine gum. The patch wasn't working." He paused. "Call me at the first sign of trouble. Not that I can do much from here."

"I feel safe now."

There was one more *snap*, then nothing.

Stuart opened the curtains a little and watched for Jeremy.

Stephen picked up his smartphone and poked it. "You can't act Amish without listening to this."

"This better not be 'Bohemian Rhapsody.'"

He shook his head and held out his phone. A YouTube video was loading.

> *As I walk through the valley where I harvest my grain,*
> *I take a look at my wife and realize she's very plain . .*

"'Amish Paradise,'" he said. "Weird Al Yankovic."

"Doesn't help."

I picked up the room phone and dialed the front desk. The old man answered.

"Do you know where we can get some Amish clothes?"

"Say what?"

I switched to my outdoor voice, the one I use when Hunter Thicke lacks understanding.

"Amish clothes. We need some. Is there some kind of store—"

"You don't need to shout. Try Amanda's Mercantile on Main Street."

"Thanks." I hung up.

"Time to go shopping," I announced.

"Who's buying?" Stuart asked, still pulling the curtain aside.

"Your turn."

"Oh, God. I hope there's a sale."

We were the only customers. The girl at the counter probably wasn't Amanda herself. Too young. Too much makeup. But at least she wore a traditional outfit. The combination was jarring.

"We close in twenty minutes," she said.

Like contestants on *Supermarket Sweep,* we took off in all directions and grabbed stuff off the racks.

"I'm glad to get rid of my shirts to keep from getting noticed, but I doubt I can find my size," Stuart said, standing in line with me to use the only dressing room.

Stephen emerged from trying things on. "What do you think?" he asked, snapping his suspenders and tipping his straw hat. "Think I'll grow a beard to go with my new wardrobe."

"Me, too," I said.

"No, seriously. How do I look?"

"Like Harrison Ford's unfortunate younger brother."

He ignored me as Stuart took his turn. When he came out, he looked like a pious Mr. Pickwick. "I can barely button up," he said. "But these are the biggest pants they've got."

"Just keep inhaling," I said.

I opened the door and tried on my outfit. I avoided looking too closely in the mirror, no thanks to Jenny Craig.

I settled for a mostly brown ensemble that would give me plenty of room for shoo-fly pie.

But not so much that Aaron might lose interest.

* * *

Ow.

Something was sticking me in the ear. I rolled over in the opposite direction, only to have more of it jab me in the face.

I sniffed. Straw.

Blinking hard, I raised my head. Turns out there was a pillow under it, full of feathers and embroidered with the words THIS IS THE DAY THAT THE LORD HATH MADE.

Slowly it all came back to me. Our first day among the Amish—Saturday.

I sat up. The first hints of orange sunrise streamed

through the barn loft window, motes of dust floating in the air. I sneezed.

Rooookaroooooarooooooh! something screeched. Raptor or rooster? The latter seemed more likely.

"*Urrrf!*" Stephen sounded strained, as if Stuart were sitting on his back. "I've had enough of farm livin'."

I looked down at the two very separate gentlemen brushing off bits of chaff. Stuart picked something out of his hair, peered and it, and dropped it like a hot tarantula.

There was a knock at the barn door. A moment later it rumbled slowly to the side. A man stuck his head in and removed his straw hat. It was Aaron.

"Sorry to bust in, but we tend to rise before the sun. The Bishop wanted me to show you around."

Stuart sneezed, then wiped his nose on his Amish sleeve. "Do you people have handkerchiefs?"

Aaron scratched his chin. "I believe Sister Stoltzfus has one, but I've never seen her use it."

"When's breakfast?" Stephen asked, rubbing his eyes.

"After chores."

Stephen picked up his pillow, punched it, and tossed it on the floorboards. "Remember, Carolyn, this was your idea."

"Remember, you didn't *have* any."

Aaron put his hat back on and cleared his throat. "There's a privy behind the barn if you need it."

"Is that what I think it is?" Stephen asked. "An outhouse?"

Aaron nodded.

Without speaking, the three of us lined up and did what had to be done. I found it resembled a gas station restroom, except that everything was wooden and there was a copy of something called *The Amish Heresy* lying next to the throne.

"So," Aaron said when we'd completed our eliminations, "let's start with a few facts. There's 110 acres here, one of the bigger farms in the county. About a hundred head of livestock—mostly cattle, poultry, and hogs. We grow melons, oilseed, sweet potatoes. Just started on Christmas trees."

He waited as if for a reaction.

"Quite a . . . spread," I said.

"You'll be doing the usual chores."

"Such as?"

"Milking, shoveling manure, feeding horses and chickens." He paused. "Unless you know how to drive a tractor or run a harvester."

We looked at each other. "Not much call for that in our neck of the woods," I said.

"Let's check the cows first." He led the way to the other side of the barn, where cattle stood in stalls, chewing their cuds—and actually *lowing*.

He reached over the stall door and patted a black one with a white diamond shape on its forehead. "This is Dorcas. My favorite. Delivered her fifth calf last spring."

Stephen coughed. "Man, that manure is pungent."

"You get used to it," Aaron said. He looked down at the floor of Dorcas' stall and frowned. "Now, that's not right."

"What's the matter?" I asked.

"Got the runs. Color's not good, either." To my surprise, he pulled a smartphone from his pocket. "Better call the doc."

Stephen held his nose. "Just like *All Creatures Great and Small*. I can hardly wait to see whether the vet shows up wearing a herringbone jacket with patches on the elbows."

Aaron turned away from the cow and described the problem on the phone. He paused, listening. "Eleven o'clock, then. We'll be here."

He turned back to us. "Okay," he said. "Since we're here, let's start with milking. Anybody done this before?"

We all shook our heads. "Some of the dairymen around here use milking machines—but with our small herd we do it the old-fashioned way."

He reached up to a nearby shelf and took down a box. "Agriculture Department wants to use rubber gloves nowadays." He gave each of us a pair of blue ones. We pulled them on, which was more of a struggle than I expected.

At the third stall he patted a sleepy-looking brown cow. "Rachel's easy to get along with. She's already secured with a rope. The key is to be gentle. They don't mind being milked if you do it right. Do it wrong, though, and you could get kicked in the head."

Stuart looked around as if trying to find an escape route.

"Carolyn, let's give you the first shot." He pointed at a three-legged stool. "Sit there and pull up a bucket."

There being no dignified way to reach the level of that stool, I dropped like a stone and almost lost my balance.

"Want to use some Bag Balm?" Aaron asked.

"Do I have to?"

"Nope." He paused. "Now strip each teat to get the bacteria out. Gently squeeze it a few times like you would a leaky tube of toothpaste."

Keeping an eye on those hooves, I did it.

"Good. Now put the bucket under the udder. Take two of the teats and gently clamp them with your fingers."

When I tried it, the poor animal started making warning sounds.

"Don't pinch," Aaron said.

I prayed a quick prayer, then squeezed as gingerly as I could.

"Just a touch harder."

I tried again.

"You got it. Now, do that until a quarter of the bag looks deflated."

Swallowing, I worked the program until he told me to quit. "Nice," he said. "Rachel would thank you, but the Lord didn't give her the power of speech."

I struggled to my feet and relinquished my post to Stuart, then Stephen. They seemed to pick it up more easily than I did. Apparently coming from Idaho wasn't enough to make you a natural.

When we were done, we moved on to less specialized tasks like shoveling manure and feeding the chickens. By then it was time for breakfast, a feast of ham with oatmeal and honey. Most of the family was already out in the fields.

After thanking the Bishop's wife, Aaron led us downstairs to the root cellar and showed us the canned goods. It looked like the shelves in a laboratory of body parts, mostly eyeballs and viscera, but of course it was cherries and berries and jams of all kinds.

"Wow," said Stuart, and sat down on a rickety-looking chair which promptly broke. Aaron helped him up.

There was an old striped mattress, no linens, in the corner. Three of us sat on it. I was next to Aaron, but tried not to look at him.

Stephen took a jar from the shelf. "Are these apricots?"

"Peaches," Aaron said.

"Mind if I try some?"

"Be my guest. But I don't have a spoon."

"No problem." He popped off the lid with his thumb and fished out half a peach with his fingers.

"Eww," I said.

"Aaron, ever heard 'Amish Paradise'?" Stephen asked.

Aaron hesitated, as if Lucifer were asking a trick question and the answer might determine his eternal destiny.

"I've heard it," he finally confessed.

"You can listen to the radio?"

Aaron held up his smartphone. "Spotify."

"We won't tell anybody," I said.

"I don't think I'm the only one. But the rest usually pray for Al Yankovic. They're more spiritual."

I looked up at the cellar's dirt ceiling. "The Lord has given us all good things to enjoy."

He nodded, but his expression was doubtful.

"Pass the peaches," I said.

* * *

Aaron rolled the barn door open after lunch. An orange truck from Home Depot drove up behind him.

"Got some four-by-fours," he said. "Fifty of 'em. Can't haul that many in a wagon."

The driver, a sunburned guy with a neck tattoo, popped out of the cab and started unloading the timbers. Aaron pulled on some leather gloves and joined him.

Stuart backed up a step. "I've got a bad feeling about this."

Aaron laughed. "Work is worship. Don't worry, you don't have to do this part. But we're going to have a hands-on lesson in sinking fence posts."

"I'm allergic to splinters," Stephen said.

"You'll find plenty of gloves in that box next to the pitchfork."

We found three pairs. They were all too big for me, and Stuart's had a dead spider in it.

Aaron and the driver made a stack of lumber the size of a Sherman tank. Aaron tipped him and he drove away. The tip surprised me, but I wasn't sure why.

"We've already got the stringers," Aaron said. "But first we have to use the post-hole digger."

He went to a corner and dragged out a tool that looked like two wheelbarrow handles with a circle of steel between them. "Some of the English have gas-powered augers for this. I think this kind builds character."

He pointed to the horizon. "Need to replace the fence and

cattle guard. We'll sink about a quarter of the posts in concrete today and more tomorrow."

We looked at each other. "There's still time to surrender to the Boudreaux family," Stephen mumbled.

"You could use some character," I said. "Maybe there'll be lemonade at the end."

He scuffed his shoe in the dirt. "Harrison Ford didn't have to do this."

"Let's go," Aaron called.

The next three hours were occupied by a form of worship I hope never to participate in again, having gotten used to the kind that did not involve physical injury. Suffice it to say that when we were done, I was covered in enough sweat and grime that I could be mistaken for a mud wrestler in the middle of the Dust Bowl.

Mrs. Stoltzfus, taking pity on me, let me use her shower. I was too grateful to ask about washers and dryers, and figured I didn't have the strength to use a washtub and hand wringer. Maybe tomorrow I could find a rock in the creek to pound my outfit on.

Stephen and Stuart were sweaty too, but couldn't seem to move. They lay on the straw in the barn, staring at their phones, their odor masked by that of the animals.

Our state of suspendered animation was interrupted by the clang of a dinner bell. We hobbled to the house. I hoped the meal would be extra fragrant to cover our multitude of sins.

Mrs. Stoltzfus met us at the door. "I could eat a horse," Stephen said.

She raised an eyebrow. "Oh, the food isn't ready yet. Carolyn, please join us in the kitchen." She looked doubtfully at Stephen and Stuart. "You can sit with the menfolk in the living room."

"Ever made chicken pot pie?" she asked me.

"Can't say I have."

"Come with me."

Four women were already chopping and mixing in the kitchen. One was lighting a massive iron wood stove. I could smell the scent of match meeting kindling.

"You can help me make the crust," the Bishop's wife said. "The secret of a flakier crust is to freeze the butter first and grate it with a cheese grater." She handed me a bowl of white stuff. "Since this is a special occasion, we're using the churned butter. Here's the grater."

I went to work, praying for my knuckles.

"I notice that only the ladies are preparing the food," I said. "Do the men ever help?"

She frowned. "They do their part."

"Which is?"

"The parts of men and women are different."

I stifled a snicker, but couldn't help smiling. "So true."

"Why are you smiling?" she asked suspiciously.

"Must be the joy of the Lord." I paused. "Still, it seems to me that in Christ there is neither male nor female."

She shook her head. "Even though the Apostle Paul could have insisted on his rights, he made himself a servant to all that he might win them."

She looked more sad than angry.

"Sorry," I said. "Overstepped my bounds."

Not speaking, she started mixing the dough. Fashioning four crusts, she called for another woman to supply the filling.

My face felt hot. I wanted to hide under the table.

Brushing flour from her hands, she sighed. "I must remind myself not to judge. Your ways and ours are simply different. Let God sort things out."

"Thank you."

She slid the pies into the oven. There was a *whoosh* as the fire flared, fed by oxygen through the open door.

Half an hour later the feast began. We all held hands as the Bishop prayed for our safety.

When I opened my eyes, I looked around at the others.

Only a few of them knew the danger they were in.

What would the rest think if they knew what he was talking about?

CHAPTER 8

The Sunday morning rooster sounded just like the Saturday one.

He crowed three times, betraying his total lack of interest in our inability to move.

"Morning," I muttered to the ceiling. I hoped the cows had the morning off.

Having worked out a system, I went to a stall to freshen up. I'd filled a bucket with cold water the night before from an outside faucet. Unless the Bishop's wife kept taking pity on me, we'd have to work on the issue of hot water later.

The rooster crowed again, apparently feeling it necessary to make an extra effort on the Lord's day.

"Shut *up!*" Stephen yelled. I could hear him rustling in the loft. A cloud of chaff drifted down, lit by the sunrise.

I assumed Stuart was still alive, despite having been forced light years out of his comfort zone. Perhaps he was even awake.

There was a rap at the door, then the sideways shove that let the day inside.

"Sabbath greetings," Aaron said, entirely too happily.

Stephen grunted. I tried to be glad when he said unto me, "Let us go in to the house of the Lord," but my joy button was stuck.

"Breakfast is served," Aaron said as proudly as if he'd made it himself—which of course he hadn't.

It was a small gathering around the Stoltzfus' table. Everyone looked solemn, dressed in their Sunday best. The men took off their hats.

The Bishop stood. "Let us pray."

Heads bowed in unison. The little assumed grand-daughter folded her hands, then looked at me as if to make sure I did, too. I followed suit.

"Mighty God, the Scriptures tell us to gather on the first day of the week to acknowledge the saving resurrection of Your Son. May the nourishment of which we are about to partake give us the strength to worship you in spirit and in truth. Amen."

"Amen," said everybody who was anybody.

The lady of the house brought in a platter of cinnamon rolls. Not the kind you get at Safeway or even Cinnabon. The real thing, buttery and frosted a quarter inch deep. I could smell them from 10 feet away, and nearly swooned.

"Yikes," Stephen said.

The Bishop's wife put her hands on her hips. "Is there a problem?"

"Only if you run out before I get one."

"I have asked my wife to explain our worship service," the Bishop said, taking the first roll.

I took the second. It was still warm from the wood stove. Stephen stared at the platter, no doubt comparing the number of diners with the number of remaining pastries.

Mrs. Stoltzfus sat down. "Most meetings are held in people's homes. On Sundays during tourist season we meet in the outdoor pavilion down the road."

"You get tourists?" I asked.

"Unfortunately, yes."

"Though we consider it an opportunity to introduce them to the gospel," the Bishop hastened to add.

Finally the plate got to Stephen. Two rolls left. Taking one, he gave a sigh of relief.

"Do you have music?" I asked.

"Oh, yes," the Bishop's wife said. "Usually in German, then English."

"But no instruments," Aaron said.

When the conversation ended, there was one roll left. Stephen eyed it like a hawk.

I leaned toward him. "It is better to give than to receive," I whispered.

"Says who?"

"Says me and at least One other."

He sank back in his chair, pouting.

The little girl folded her hands across her chest. "I think we should give the last roll to Grandma. She made them."

Mrs. Stoltzfus shook her head, then nodded at Stephen. "Mr. Ames, isn't it?"

His eyes widened. "Yes."

"Man shall not live by bread alone, but by every word that proceeds from the mouth of God."

"Um . . . okay."

"I cannot give you the Bread of life, but I can give you this roll. Can you acknowledge that it comes from the Lord's hand?"

He swallowed hard. "I guess so."

"Then take it with my blessing."

He put it on his plate. Taking a knife, he cut it in half and gave the rest to the little girl. "Give it to anyone you like."

She looked around, her face sober. Finally she gave it to Aaron. "He works hard," she said.

Aaron grinned. "Want some?" he asked me.

"I'm full. And she's right."

The Bishop looked at the antique clock on the wall. "Let's go, shall we?"

Aaron ate the rest of the roll in three bites and washed it down with coffee. We all rose and followed the Bishop out the door.

Like the children of Israel, we marched down the road to the pavilion. It was fashioned of hand-hewn logs, mostly open on the sides. I could imagine Noah building something similar, though he'd have done it in more of a hurry.

Aaron led us to the third row. The back was full of tourists sneaking pictures of the "plain people" with their phones, probably not realizing that most of the younger ones used the devices themselves.

"Testing. Testing." A baby-faced blond man of about 30, his beard almost transparent, stood in front of a microphone."

"They have a sound system?" Stephen asked, incredulous.

"It's new," Aaron said. "For the convenience of our guests, of course. Not everyone agreed, but after a season of fasting the Bishop made the decision."

Mr. Stoltzfus went to the front and prayed an invocation.

"Welcome to our guests. And now, as is our custom, let us pause for silent prayer and meditation."

Heads bowed. I tried to concentrate on my parents and persecuted Christians in China, but kept thinking of Jeremy and the Nameless Girl instead.

It seemed to take forever. I could feel Stephen squirming next to me.

At last the Bishop cleared his throat. When you don't have any instruments, it's hard to make a smooth transition, I guess.

He set a huge Bible on the pulpit, opened it, and began to preach.

"Let it please the Holy Spirit, our subject this morning is staying true to Christ and the Order." After reading a passage from Philippians, he began.

I have long believed most sermons should be shorter, and this one did not alter that conviction. I began to doze off after half an hour or so. Stephen and Stuart didn't last quite that long. The dear Bishop was sincere, but could have put a whole sanctuary full of Eutychuses to sleep.

I'm not sure when, but a blast of microphone feedback shocked me awake. The Bishop was closing his Bible.

"Thank God that's over," Stephen whispered.

But it was only the beginning. The baby-faced guy got up, opened his own Bible, and explained he was a deacon. Then he launched into the second half of a double feature.

Stuart and Stephen looked at each other. I could swear I saw tears in their eyes.

The deacon, God bless him, probably had a spiritual gift. This wasn't it.

If only a woman were allowed to speak, I thought. Not me, but somebody.

On the other hand, I'd already learned it wasn't my place to change this particular corner of the world.

When the exhortation ended, they sang "There is a Balm in Gilead"—first in German, then English. I could remember hearing it as a girl at home, on a record by Mahalia Jackson.

> *There is a balm in Gilead*
> *To make the wounded whole*
> *There is a balm in Gilead*
> *To save a sin-sick soul.*
> *If you cannot preach like Peter*
> *If you cannot preach like Paul*

Oh, you can tell the love of Jesus
You can say He died for us all . . .

When the service finally finished, there was much hand-shaking. Stuart and Stephen rubbed their lower backs and groaned about having to sit for so long.

The tourists got into their cars and drove away. Most of the congregation left, followed by my colleagues.

I lingered, approaching Aaron and another young man who were unplugging the sound system. "Can I help?" I asked.

Aaron scratched his chin. "Not that I know of."

I looked around. The hymnals were still on the seats. I started collecting them and stacking them up.

"That's man's work," he said. "But I can't stop you, can I?"

He gave me one of those shy smiles.

"Not if you know what's good for you," I said.

* * *

For the next three days I checked in with ex-agent Gallagher every morning after breakfast. He was on the move.

He was off the wagon, though, when it came to cigarettes. I could tell because he sounded so relaxed. No snapping at me, no snapping that obnoxious gum.

"I'm a new man," he said, then went into a coughing fit.

"Congratulations. I'll be sure to quote you at your funeral."

He cleared his throat so loudly I had to hold my phone away from my head. "I'm about twelve hours away. Is there a place to stay where you are?"

"Yeah. It's called a barn."

"Not interested. I'm thinking more of a motel."

"There's one down the road. Not exactly the Holiday Inn."

"I'll get a room in case somebody from the family discovers where you are. If that happens, I'll try to get backup. I've still got a few contacts at the FBI, but managed to alienate most of them with my so-called Boudreaux obsession."

"What are they going to do, sweep in like a SWAT team? How far away are they?"

"Three hours, maybe."

"And in the meantime, what do we do?"

"Pray to heaven and run like—"

"These people are in danger. I wake up every morning worrying we're all going to end up as the latest mass shooting on the national news."

"Ma'am, as I recall this wasn't my idea."

"I know, it was stupid. But at the time it seemed better than a shooting involving just three of us."

"What are you doing there, anyway? Sitting around in a barn, eating watermelon and summer sausage?"

I had a mind to press the END button, but figured we might need him later. "Of the three of us, I've gained a reputation for being the least incompetent outsider when it comes to making beef jerky. Stephen consumes it in disturbing amounts. I'm afraid he's going to die of colon cancer."

"Is that it?"

"Stuart's still nervous, but he learned how to drive a tractor. Nearly ran down a deacon in the bean field yesterday. Tried to make up for it by offering to draw a caricature of him."

"Doesn't sound like a fair trade. Especially if you think making a picture of yourself sucks the soul out of you."

I closed my eyes. "No, no. That's not what they believe. It's about graven . . . . Never mind. Let's just say the deacon politely declined."

"Whatever." He paused. "I'll call when I get there, okay?" He started hacking again just before the line went dead.

There was a knock at the open barn door. "Sister Neville?"

The Bishop stuck his head in. He looked as tired as I felt.

"I wonder if I might have a word with you."

I swallowed. I'd been sent to the principal's office once in fifth grade for mouthing off to the teacher. This felt the same, only worse.

He sat down on a bale of hay. I found a three-legged stool.

"It's about Brother Aaron."

"Is he . . . all right?"

"Oh, yes, yes. It's a spiritual matter."

Uh-oh.

"Not to pry, but it's obvious that he is . . . interested in you."

"Really?"

"I may be an old man, but the doctor tells me my vision is 20/20 when I'm not trying to read."

"Aaron seems to be a fine young man."

He nodded. "But even the Amish have hormones."

My face was getting hot. "I haven't tried to—"

"I know. But being a shepherd requires me to guard the members of my flock."

"Does that make me a wolf?"

He almost smiled. "Of course not. I just want you to know that Aaron is all too human. And whatever you and he may have in common, it is not wise to be unequally yoked."

I started to protest that I, too, was a Christian, but knew deep down that we were miles apart in other ways.

I sighed. "You're a wise man."

"The fear of the Lord is the beginning of wisdom. I'm just getting started." He rose slowly to his feet. "I trust you'll ponder these things in your heart."

"I promise."

He touched the brim of his straw hat, turned, and trudged toward the farmhouse.

He was right. I had to stop acting like an infatuated teenager.

Next time Aaron and I talked, it would have to be about the danger we faced.

* * *

We met after dinner in a grove of white pines, where the gravel drive met the highway. In Stephen's absence, Aaron identified the species and told me the tallest tree in Lancaster County was one of these, 128 feet. They seemed to grow in all directions, an army of bristling creatures that reminded me of *Swamp Thing*. But I digress.

The sun had dropped behind the purple hills, with just enough afterglow to conceal the stars. I could see the lights of surrounding villages.

We stood a respectable six feet apart, no hand holding. I shivered a little.

"You know, I haven't been entirely honest with you," I said.

He raised an eyebrow and waited.

"I said we were here on a spiritual retreat. The truth is we're hiding."

"From what?"

"Some people who are trying to kill Stuart. And the rest of us."

He took a step back. "By 'the rest of us,' what do you mean?"

"Mainly Stephen and me. But these people aren't particular. The whole community could be in danger."

"Why do they want to kill Stuart?"

"He's got a gambling problem. He borrowed too much, and now he can't pay it back."

"So they're loan sharks."

It was my turn to raise an eyebrow. "You know about those?"

"I may be old-fashioned, but I haven't been locked in the root cellar for the last thirty years."

"Point taken."

"Why are you putting your lives on the line for Stuart?"

"We're friends. Business acquaintances, but a little more—at least in my case. Besides, these criminals are after us, too."

"But he seems a bit . . . different."

"How?"

He looked at the gathering shadows on the ground. "He's . . . well . . . not a normal man."

"Neither is Stephen."

"Probably not, but he's more . . ."

"Overweight?"

He shook his head, clearly wishing he hadn't brought up the subject.

"The Scripture calls it *effeminate*, I believe."

"Ah. *Gay*."

"Sorry to offend you. I suppose we're not all of the same mind in this matter."

I sighed. "I'll allow that the Bible is fairly clear. But what about the grace of Christ?"

He looked up. The stars were finally visible.

"We are so small. I shouldn't judge. But hasn't the Lord spoken?"

"Aaron, for some reason God has allowed us to be in the line of fire, and our pursuers don't care who we're attracted to."

He nodded.

"The Bishop has known about the danger since we got

here. I'm surprised he agreed to this arrangement, but he did."

He picked up a stone and flung it toward the horizon. "It's a test, perhaps, or a way to remind us how little we miss by not following the ways of the world."

"Maybe. All I know is we have to be on our guard."

We stood there, listening. The sounds of civilization, like motors, were nonexistent. There was a chirping in the tall grass.

"Camel crickets," he said.

"Getting dark. We'd better go."

We walked back toward the barn, still not holding hands.

A pair of headlights flashed from behind us, lighting up the trees. An engine churning. Car coming down the road.

"Get out of sight," I whispered.

We sprinted into the trees, the grass whipping my ankles. The white pines were slender, but crowded together. Doing our best to hide behind the trunks, we waited for the car to pass.

It was hard to make out, but not a white Cadillac. Something smaller, maybe brown.

I saw the profile of a young woman at the wheel.

"Could be the Nameless Girl," I whispered.

"Who?"

"I'll explain later."

Taking out my phone, I hit Gallagher's number.

There was no answer.

CHAPTER 9

BACK AT THE BARN, STEPHEN WAS WATCHING SOMETHING ON his phone. Not sure what it was, but I kept hearing a grating tune from something called *The Itchy and Scratchy Show*.

Stuart was pacing, wearing an oval in the straw. His hands were in his pockets. Didn't look all that effeminate, but what did I know?

"We're leaving," I announced, grabbing my trash bag of belongings.

Stuart looked up. "Why?"

"I think the Nameless Girl is here."

Stephen dropped his phone. "It's too soon! I thought we had two weeks!"

The sound of an engine grew louder outside, then stopped.

Stuart and Stephen hefted their trash bags. Stephen picked up his phone, blew off the chaff, and stuffed it in his pocket.

Looking around, Aaron found a pitchfork on the wall. After yanking it from its bracket, he tapped the tines on the floor. Bits of dried manure fell away.

"Oh, baby," Stephen said. "Just what we need."

"I can't do more than threaten anybody with it," Aaron said, watching the door. "Violence isn't our way."

"Better than nothing," I whispered. "Let's go."

By the light of a single bulb we formed a caravan and snuck out the back. The smell of fertilizer vanished as we moved into the fresh air.

"Into the car," I said.

I was about to push the unlock button on the fob when I froze.

Silhouetted against the moon was the Nameless Girl, a pistol in her hand.

* * *

The back screen door of the Stoltzfus house flew open with a bang. The Bishop's wife stepped out, a rolling pin in her hand.

"What's going on?" she called.

The Nameless Girl aimed at her.

"She's got nothing to do with this," I said. "Your argument's with Stuart. And us."

The young woman flicked off the safety. "Lady, my argument's with *everybody*."

There was a growl on my right. I turned to see Aaron toss the pitchfork aside. Apparently the threat hadn't worked. Like they say, never bring a farm implement to a gunfight.

He trotted toward her. I couldn't imagine what he was going to do; a good Amish boy would never strike a woman, English or not.

Stephen, unconstrained by such values, spat in the dirt. Picking up the pitchfork, he proceeded to fling it like a javelin but missed. It knocked the gun from her hand, then nearly grazed Mrs. Stoltzfus and stuck in the side of the house like William Tell's arrow with a *chuck* sound.

The Nameless Girl snickered. "You throw like a girl, dipweed." She walked toward the pistol.

I dropped my purse on the driveway, pepper spray not being my weapon of choice in this situation, and asked myself what Harrison Ford would do.

"You're the dipweed, sister," I said, trying to sound like I knew what I was doing. Which of course I didn't.

She snorted. "What are you going to do, diss me to death?"

Remembering my brief and undistinguished career in tenth grade P.E. as a flag football player, I launched myself in her direction.

Head down and reaching out, I tackled her in the midsection. We hit the ground like a couple of hissing ferrets fighting for the alpha female spot.

What was I thinking? She was probably 15 years younger than I, not to mention the muscles and the cool leather jacket. I found myself with my cheek in the dirt, breathless.

Keeping her knee on the side of my neck, she edged toward the gun. "You're pathetic," she said.

Suddenly a manure-encrusted boot descended and pinned her arm to the ground.

"Sorry," Aaron said. "You leave me no choice. 'When the strong man guards his own house, his goods are safe.' From Luke, chapter eleven."

He nodded at Stephen. "Perhaps you could take the weapon."

"Thought you'd never ask."

The Nameless Girl writhed in the dust.

"*Crap*," she said, only it was something much worse.

* * *

In no hurry to get up, I spit out the grit and watched a cricket hop past my nose. Ah, to be one of God's less complicated creatures.

Aaron carefully took his boot from the young woman's neck and held down both of her arms with his hands. "I'd help you up, Carolyn, but I'm a little busy."

I looked at Stephen. "I know you've got that heavy artillery to hold, but maybe you could spare a second." I lifted my hand from the dirt, noticing I'd managed to break a nail.

He reached down and, keeping his eye on the girl, helped me to my feet. "Have you considered joining G.L.O.W.?"

"Who?"

"Gorgeous Ladies of Wrestling. Fictional, of course. Netflix series."

I wobbled a little. "If it's fictional, how can I join?"

"Well . . there's an actual Women's Wrestling Association."

I shook my head. "Can't afford to break more than one nail."

"I swear you've got what it takes."

Speaking of swearing, the Nameless Girl chose that moment to prove once again she excelled in that department. My ears didn't burn. Just smoldered a little.

Deciding to speed-dial Gallagher, I fished my phone from my purse. No bars.

"Stuart," I yelled. "Call Gallagher, will you?"

He still looked dazed. "Uh . . . sure."

I gave him the number. He was starting to punch it in when the rest of the Stoltzfus family poured from the house.

"Good Lord," cried the Bishop.

Aaron tried to appear less entangled with his prisoner, but only succeeded in looking like a 19th century Twister player.

The Bishop walked to the barn, then returned with a length of fat sisal rope. "Let all of you be witness. I do this with great reluctance, begging divine forgiveness should it be necessary."

Stuart gasped. "You're not going to *hang* her, are you?"

The old man's eyes widened. "God forbid. I only wish to learn from our Lord's observation in Mark 3:27, the verse about binding the strong man."

He scratched his beard, remembering. "'No man can enter into a strong man's house and despoil his goods, unless he will first bind the strong man; and then he will despoil his house.' Not prescriptive, of course, but descriptive."

"Whatever," Stephen said, still holding the gun.

"Also a bit out of context," the Bishop continued. "Yet I believe the grace of Christ will allow it under the circumstances."

He and Aaron tied the rope around the woman's wrists and feet. Fortunately, it was long enough to keep her from looking like a trussed-up Thanksgiving turkey.

I found a bale of straw and sat, breathing a sigh of relief.

"What's that?" the Bishop's granddaughter asked, pointing down the driveway.

"Oh, *double* crap," Stephen muttered.

Another car was pulling up.

A white Cadillac.

The white Cadillac.

CHAPTER 10

I STOOD UP, SEARCHING FOR A PLACE TO RUN. THERE wasn't any.

"*Triple* crap," Stephen said. He wheeled to face the car.

"I'll take the gun," I said.

"But—"

"You look a little too desperate. Desperate people do surprisingly unpleasant things."

Frowning, he handed it over. I pointed it at my recent wrestling partner.

The Cadillac's door opened. Out climbed Jeremy, oilier than usual. His gun was bigger, too.

He looked down. "You must be the new girl." He shook his head. "I hope they don't expect me to train you."

She swore again. He just chuckled.

"Hey, Jethro," he said, glancing at Aaron. "Untie the lady."

Having abandoned his game of Twister, Aaron sighed and took a penknife from his pocket.

Jeremy stepped closer. "Try to use that for anything other than rope and you'll be dangling from the rafters yourself."

Aaron sawed away at the woman's bonds. "I understand," he mumbled.

Mr. Oilyface turned to me. "I'll take the gun, Sweetheart."

Yeah, I could picture Dwight Schrute saying that. Only Dwight would be armed with a stapler.

I handed over the weapon. One of the Stoltzfus girls was crying softly. The Bishop's wife put her arm around her.

Jeremy sauntered over to Stuart, who was hiding in the shadows. "Got the money, Mr. Lytle?"

"No. But—"

"Time's up."

He turned to the Bishop. "I bet Farmer Brown here's got some cash. Where do you guys hide your money, under a mattress?"

"I am reminded of a verse from the Book of Acts: 'Silver and gold have I none; but such as I have give I thee.'"

Jeremy cocked his head to one side. "So what have you got?"

"Forgiveness."

"Not interested."

The Bishop sighed. "Sometimes we want least what we need most."

"What I need least is a sermon from you."

"God will be the judge."

"Great." He paused, then looked back at Stuart. "My employer's been very patient but even he has his limits. His competitors notice the slightest sign of weakness."

"If I just had another couple of weeks—"

Ignoring him, Jeremy tossed the young woman's gun in her direction. Aaron cut the last bit of rope. She sat up, grabbed the weapon, and kicked him in the side of the head.

"*Ooh,*" said Jeremy. "Jethro, that's gotta hurt."

Aaron said nothing, but looked dazed.

Jeremy raised his firearm and took aim at Stuart.

"You farm folk turn around. No need to see this."

The Bishop closed his eyes, probably praying. His wife took their granddaughter by the shoulders and marched her back into the house.

"Next time, Stuart, don't make bets you can't cover," Jeremy said.

I tried not to look Stuart in the eye. There would be no next time, and he knew it.

* * *

Another car door shut on the other side of the house. I could hear gravel crunching under somebody's shoes.

Jeremy and the Nameless Girl whirled toward the sound.

"Lay down on the ground, Stuart," Jeremy ordered.

The crunching stopped. There was a rustling in the bushes.

"Whoever you are, this isn't a good time," Jeremy called, gripping the butt of his gun with both hands. He aimed at the foliage. "Dare you to show your face."

The young woman took cover behind the corner of the barn. The Bishop's eyes were still shut.

A gunshot exploded from somewhere in the greenery. The young woman hissed, then swore again. Stumbling from her hiding place, she held her shoulder.

Gun pointed at the sky, Jeremy dashed toward me. "Get down," he told the girl. "God, don't you know anything?"

I froze. He grabbed me, bent his arm around my neck, and squeezed. I couldn't recall being a human shield before. The harder he squeezed, the less I could see. Sparks of color danced at the edges of my peripheral vision.

A figure rose from the bushes like Botticelli's Venus from the giant clamshell. This one was clothed, though, in a ratty tan raincoat Columbo would be proud of. And armed with a gun that probably required a special permit.

It was Gallagher.

"Put down your weapons!" he barked.

The cavalry had come after all. But the odds were anything but promising.

"Is that you, Gallagher?" Jeremy asked, incredulous. "You've really let yourself go. Aren't you a little too old for this sort of thing?"

"Aren't you a little too stupid?" the former agent called. "Two of us. One of you. Sounds pretty dumb to me."

"The FBI is on its way."

Mr. Oilyface gave a cynical laugh. "Bullcrap."

Gallagher raised his gun and fired. With a POP the sodium lamp illuminating the barnyard shattered. The only light left was a kerosene lantern in the window of the house.

Swearing, Jeremy released his grip and waved his weapon blindly at the shadows.

It was now or never. I pulled away, my neck throbbing.

In the half-dark I could barely make out Aaron's profile. He seemed to be picking up the rope and slinking toward Jeremy.

"What the—" Jeremy cried. Aaron tripped him, sending him into a badly executed cartwheel. His gun went flying.

The dark shape of Stephen leapt forward, picked up the sidearm, and flung it into the woods.

"Good time to surrender," Gallagher said, and coughed.

"You're forgetting something," Jeremy said, panting on the ground. "My colleague, inept as she may be, is still armed." He paused. "You *are*, right?"

"Yeah, but—"

I helped Stuart up. "This way," I whispered, then dragged him toward Stephen.

A shot rang out, the bullet zipping past my ear. The

Nameless Girl's aim might be a little off, but not enough to give me any comfort.

"Stephen, follow us," I said, and led them toward the car.

* * *

Jeremy got up, swaying like a drunk, a trickle of blood running down his forehead. Staggering toward the trees, he squinted at the darkness. Apparently he was looking for the gun.

He tripped over something but caught himself at the last second. His profanity was half-hearted, or maybe just exhausted.

Gallagher coughed again. "Like I said, a good time to—"

Another POP, and it was Gallagher's turn to curse.

"Thanks for letting me know where you are," the Nameless Girl called.

"Missed me," he said. "And that works both ways."

A shot sounded from his direction. She cried out in pain.

A member of the Stoltzfus clan finally switched on the porch light. I could see the young woman limping to her car, still holding her shoulder.

"*Now*," I whispered, herding Stephen and Stuart in the opposite direction.

We scrambled toward the car. Jeremy gave up his search among the trees and turned toward us, his eyes cold. He checked his gun to make sure he wasn't out of ammo.

Gallagher stepped into the light and popped something in his mouth. Cough drop, maybe.

"Ms. Neville, I'll take it from here."

"God be with you!" the Bishop called, looking one-fourth worried and three-fourths glad to be rid of us.

Aaron waved sadly. I wondered whether I'd see him again.

Swallowing, I got behind the wheel and turned the key. I could hear Stephen and Stuart slam their doors and buckle their seatbelts.

I waved back.

Then I drove into the night, the tires spitting gravel.

CHAPTER 11

"Wow," Stephen said. "The first Amish action hero."

"Who?" I asked.

"Aaron. Like to see what he could do with Harrison Ford's bullwhip."

"Where are we going?" Stuart asked, sounding shell-shocked.

"God only knows," I said.

There was nothing in the rearview mirror. I eased my foot off the accelerator, slowing from 65 to 50. The last speed limit sign I'd seen said 45.

"We've got about a quarter of a tank. That should take us somewhere."

Stephen took out his phone. "I'm gonna check for the nearest major highway and gas station."

Stuart cleared his throat. "Carolyn, I'm glad you feel the Almighty knows where we're going, but He and I aren't on speaking terms."

"I'm open to suggestion."

There was a long silence.

"I wonder what Gallagher's going to do," Stuart said, looking out the window.

"I doubt the FBI is on its way," I said. "I'd give him a fifty-fifty chance of holding off Jeremy and what's-her-face."

"Let's go to Mexico," Stephen said, still looking at his phone. "I speak a little Spanish."

"God, no," Stuart said. "If I wanted to live in the middle of a drug war, I'd move to Los Angeles."

"Okay. How about Idaho? We could stay with Carolyn's family. It's in the middle of nowhere."

I laughed. "You don't know my parents. They'd drive you nuts. Besides, the Boudreauxs will have all our families under surveillance."

"All we've got is the shirts on our backs," Stuart said. "I didn't even have time to bring my trash bag."

"Join the club."

Stephen looked up from his phone. "There's a Sunoco station off Highway 30."

"Where's Highway 30?"

"About ten miles from here, take a right. Exit 124."

Stuart leaned forward. "About my trash bag—"

"Definitely high priority," I said. "Or it would be, if we weren't being chased by the mob. Assuming Gallagher didn't put them out of commission."

Stuart made a frustrated noise. "You know, when I write a book I like to know what's going to happen at least a page in advance. I have this card system. You put a plot point on each card, then thumbtack them all to a cork board on the wall and keep moving them around until—"

I glanced in the mirror. "Stuart, they have computer programs for that now. And that only works for fiction. We don't get to control real life."

"So I noticed."

"For now let's have two goals: Fill the gas tank and keep driving until it's empty."

* * *

We had about three gallons left when we got to the Sunoco station.

"Who has to go?" I asked.

Stephen and Stuart raised their hands.

"I feel stupid dressed in this Amishwear," Stephen said.

"So do I," Stuart said. "Conspicuous."

I opened my door. "Maybe they sell swimsuits. Or football jerseys. But I doubt it."

We went inside to get the restroom keys. The clerk was chubbier than Stuart, pale as a bean sprout. I figured from the Civil War cap on his balding head he was one of those people who wore costumes on weekends and toasted their breakfast burritos over a campfire. At least he wasn't a Confederate.

He stared. "Didn't think you folks could drive," he said.

"Only in emergencies," I replied.

He nodded, apparently uninterested in the details.

"Sell any clothes here?" Stephen asked.

The clerk pointed at a display of clear plastic ponchos on the counter.

Stephen sighed. "Not quite what I had in mind."

The keys were attached to hunks of wood with MEN and WOMEN on them. "Don't worry, we'll buy something," I promised. "And we're filling up."

Passing a rack of food so junky it would be better used as packing material than sustenance, I came to the door with the stick-lady symbol and unlocked it.

Out of respect for the Sunoco people, but mostly for legal reasons, I must point out that what followed was no doubt unusual, perhaps due to the clerk's desire to recreate nine-teenth-century hygiene.

In four words, the place was filthy. The toilet did flush, however, even though the indoor plumbing was an anachro-nism. Since paper towels had not been invented, I used the hem of my historically accurate dress.

Returning the key, I resisted the urge to offer the clerk a review. I paid for the gas and purchased coffee, a granola bar, and a jumbo bottle of hand sanitizer.

Stephen was already consuming his big bag of Cheetos and blue Slurpee. Stuart was swallowing half an overpriced vial of Tylenol with a Big Gulp Diet Pepsi.

Back at the pump I squeegeed bugs from the windshield and watched traffic for a white Cadillac or whatever the "new girl" was driving. I didn't see either.

We got in the car. "That bathroom was the pits," Stephen said. "I'm going on Yelp."

Stuart leaned back in his seat and closed his eyes. "Wake me when we get . . . wherever we're going."

I ate the granola bar with the coffee, the latter tasting like hot iodine. "Anybody want Cheetos?" Stephen asked.

Stuart started to snore. I shook my head and pulled into traffic.

I wanted to ask for a Tylenol, but didn't have the heart to wake him up.

* * *

We drove in silence for at least 15 minutes. The coffee, disgusting as it was, kept me awake.

Finally Stephen spoke. "Love your plan," he said. "What is it again?"

"A work in progress."

He shook the last Cheeto crumbs into his mouth. "I like progress. Let's make some."

I sighed. "I think in a couple of hours we should get off the interstate and find a place to stay for the night."

He took out his phone. "How many stars you want this place to have?"

"We can only afford two. But it's got to have locks on the doors."

He poked away at the screen. "You okay with Motel Six?"

"I hear they've repented and leave the light on for all races, creeds, and colors."

"We'll get to one in just under three hours."

I grunted. "Worth waiting for, I'm sure."

He settled back in his seat and soon joined Stuart in the Land of Nod. Their combined snores were more powerful than caffeine.

After about an hour of driving, I saw a REST STOP sign. The state of Pennsylvania was looking out for me, though I hoped God was looking harder.

After refilling my water bottle at the drinking fountain, I got back in the car.

"Anybody need to use the bathroom?" I asked loudly.

Making irritated noises, Stephen and Stuart stretched and opened their doors without speaking. They walked back to the building, one with rock columns in front and a sharply pitched roof on top.

Yawning, I took out my phone and punched in Gallagher's number.

No answer. Not even voice mail.

I shivered. Maybe he hadn't made it.

Looking in the rearview mirror, I saw a car rolling into the parking lot. The lights were too bright to identify it.

I couldn't take chances. Called Stephen's number.

"Yeah? What?" He sounded ticked.

"You and Stuart have to get back to the car. *Right now*."

"I'm in the middle of something."

I wanted to scream, but just shrieked instead. "Hurry *up!*"

The headlights behind me went out. The car door opened.

The driver stepped into the light.

It was Jeremy. No sunglasses now.

I started the car.

He stepped closer. Sending up a quick prayer, I threw it into reverse.

There being little a compact can do to a barge-like Caddy, I aimed for Jeremy.

Not being suicidal, he sprang out of the way.

I looked at the restroom. Stephen, still zipping his pants, burst out the door first. Stuart followed, barely keeping up. They scrambled into the car.

Gunfire erupted. The back window shattered, raining bits of glass on the back seat. Stephen and Stuart sheltered their heads with their arms.

"What are you waiting for?" Stephen cried.

"I'm *not*," I said, and floored it onto the highway.

CHAPTER 12

Soon as I could, I made a U-turn.

"I wasn't finished," Stuart whispered.

"With what?" I asked.

"The thing I went in the restroom to do."

I glanced at the mirror and hit the gas. "Not my problem."

He fidgeted.

"We could stop and take care of it behind a tree," Stephen said.

"See that glass all over the back seat? Plenty more where that came from."

Stuart looked out his window. "Did we lose Jeremy?"

"Who knows? At this rate, he'd have to—"

Suddenly a high-pitched wail sounded behind us.

"Oh, crap," I said. A pair of stuttering blue lights flashed in the mirror.

I hadn't been pulled over since that time I got caught doing my makeup on the thruway into Manhattan. Officer said I'd been driving distracted. I made the mistake of correcting him: "Distracted-*ly*."

He'd shown his appreciation with a $75 ticket. I showed

mine by paying the fine in quarters I'd collected, each in penance for an undeserved donut or word I should have left unspoken.

Now, groaning, I pulled over.

Walking toward us was a sheriff's deputy, wearing one of those Mountie hats and a leather jacket. He reminded me of Conan O'Brien's sidekick, Andy Richter, pudgy but with an unstable streak.

"License and registration," he said.

"They're in my purse."

"Good hiding place. Would you mind *getting them out?*"

I handed them over, watching for Jeremy.

"What's with the busted window, Ma'am?"

"Somebody shot it out," Stephen volunteered. "Trying to kill us."

The cop narrowed his eyes. "Care to tell me about it?"

I pondered whether the truth would hurt. Us, that is.

Stuart leaned forward. "He's kidding, officer."

I gave him a look.

"Better safe than sorry," he whispered.

"This happen recently?" asked the deputy.

"Yeah, pretty much."

"You've gotta get it fixed."

"Soon as I can."

He tore the ticket from his pad. "Hope you can afford it."

I looked at the fine. "Not after this."

"Got some plastic you can cover it with?"

I sighed. "No."

"Well, you can't keep going with it that way. Stop as soon as possible. Get it fixed in the morning."

He returned to his car and drove off.

"I still need to go," Stuart said. The urgency in his voice was poignant.

I put the ticket in my purse and closed my eyes. "Find a

tree."

He searched the landscape. "Too close to traffic. Maybe down the road."

I started the car. "Remind me never to play miniature golf with you again."

* * *

Heading west, I kept checking the rearview mirror for the Cadillac. Stuart brushed glass shards onto the floor with his straw hat and made urgent noises.

Just as the noises were graduating to agonized groans, Stephen spotted a likely-looking tree. Mercifully, he didn't bother to identify it.

I pulled onto the shoulder. While we waited for Stuart to do what had to be done, I undid my seat belt and turned around.

"Can you find the most unlikely place for us to stay within the next hundred miles?"

"There's a Motel Six coming up, remember?"

"I'm having second thoughts."

He scratched his chin. "How about a foxhole? Or a lean-to made of sticks?"

"You're getting colder."

He took out his phone.

"Here are three other places rated even lower."

"Too obvious," I said.

Stuart knocked on his door, which had somehow gotten locked. I pushed the button on mine.

"Anybody have hand sanitizer?"

I rummaged around in my purse. The bottle was next to the pepper spray.

"Thanks," he said, and climbed in.

"Okay," said Stephen. "Here's something different. One of

those family camping places that has cabins. Couple miles off the highway. About fifteen minutes from here."

"Does this have anything to do with Yogi Bear?"

"Jellystone Park? No. Huckleberry Acres."

"Is there a picture of Huckleberry Hound? Blue guy, weird hat."

He shook his head. "How could there be two campground franchises based on Hanna-Barbara cartoons?"

I opened my mouth to tell him what a terrible idea the whole thing was, but he forged ahead.

"This place also has teepees. Rustic. Refreshments. Pony rides."

I cringed. I loved camping as much as I loved bleeding ulcers.

"Do they have yurts?" Stuart asked, clicking his seat belt.

Stephen leaned back. "Is that a disease, like shingles? Or kind of like yogurt or tofu?"

"No, it's Mongolian. Think Genghis Khan. Tent. Round. Animal skin. Like a teepee with no point. Stayed in one once. Hot as you-know-what, but had a table and chairs. Sort of a cloth bungalow, but with—"

"We get the idea," I said.

"This doesn't say anything about yurts," Stephen said.

I raised a hand. "For the sake of full disclosure, I hate camping of all kinds."

"So do I," Stuart said. But I can't think of a less likely place —except maybe a treehouse or cave."

He stuck his hand over my seat. "Here. The rest of my Tylenol."

I'd save it for later. Things were bound to get worse.

I took out my phone and tried once more to call Gallagher. Voice mail again.

Figuring it was too dangerous to leave a message, I pushed the END button.

"Camping, here we come," I said without enthusiasm.

I was smarter than the average bear.

And I'd always wanted a pony ride.

* * *

The arrow pointing toward Huckleberry Acres needed repainting.

It hung from a grinning, billboard-sized cowboy who looked suspiciously like Woody from *Toy Story* sitting on a pony that resembled a dog. The Lincoln Log lettering was faded, chipped.

Darkness veiled the long dirt driveway. Four teepees stood against the moon like 1950s-style rockets on a launchpad.

The parking lot had three dusty sedans and a camper in it. The red neon sign in the office window said VACANCY. I couldn't imagine it saying otherwise.

The car stopped, which woke my companions up. They grunted, though not quite in unison.

I peered through the windshield. "Doesn't look like rain. Which is good, since we don't have anything to patch the rear window with."

We walked wearily into the office. Empty.

Checking my watch, I was surprised it was 11:38 p.m. Felt later.

A brass cowbell sat on the counter. I picked it up. When I tried to ring it, there was only a faint clanking sound.

From the back room emerged a yawning college-age girl in pajamas and robe so puffy they obscured any anatomical details that might have made the place less than family-friendly. Her long, dark brown hair needed a brush.

She seemed startled when she saw our outfits. I couldn't blame her.

Frowning, Stephen slipped his thumbs behind his suspenders. "Does thee have a cabin?"

I cleared my throat conspicuously.

"Make that two," he said.

The girl rubbed her eyes and named a price. "Checkout time's 11 a.m. No pets, no smoking." She paused. "Do you people smoke those corncob pipe thingies?"

"We're trying to quit," Stephen said solemnly.

Sighing, I paid with a credit card.

"You sell toothbrushes?" I asked.

The clerk nodded and pointed at a pegboard below the front desk. I chose a child-sized model with a tiny tube of no-name toothpaste. Stuart did the same. Three bucks apiece.

"I'm good," Stephen said, picking Cheetos from his teeth with a toothpick he'd found in a mug on the desk.

I was too tired to shudder.

Our cabins were marked Six and Seven. Easy to find, thanks to the giant numbers made of orange reflective tape.

The decor was rustic, all right. Most of the furniture looked like it was from the Three Little Pigs Collection, fashioned of sticks. A beat-up leather saddle hung on the wall.

I pushed on my mattress. No sharp objects poked through the army green blanket.

After locking the door, I dragged a small chest of drawers in front of it. Until I replenished my wardrobe, I wouldn't need it for anything else.

I brushed my teeth. The water tasted like chlorine.

Sitting on the bed, I set my purse on the nightstand. I counted my blessings, but ran out after four. Don't recall what they were, but this time Stephen and Stuart weren't on the list.

I fell into bed. The blanket was scratchy.

Despite my better judgment, I went to sleep.

CHAPTER 13

NEXT MORNING I WOKE TO THE SOUND OF POUNDING. AFTER rolling out of bed I got dressed and went to the door, then regretted having pushed the chest of drawers against it. With a grunt I moved the furniture aside.

Squinting against the sun, I spotted a workman on a ladder, hammering one pole into another. One of the teepees had collapsed.

"Morning," called a voice to my right. It was Stephen, sipping coffee from a Styrofoam cup.

"It was empty," he said. "The wigwam, I mean."

He raised his cup as if toasting the start of a wonderful day. "The concession stand's got breakfast. Well, stuff like coffee and muffins."

I rubbed my eyes. "Donuts?"

"Yeah, I think so."

I looked at our car, wondering whether any birds or raccoons had taken up residence inside. My stomach growled. I'd investigate later.

The person in charge of refreshments was almost too short to see over the counter. She could have been the desk clerk's little sister, maybe ten years old. First person I'd seen in red pigtails since they updated the logo at Wendy's.

"Help you?" she asked.

"Are the donuts good?"

She shrugged. "Depends."

"On what?"

"On what day it is. We get 'em from a place in town. Wednesday's raspberry. Got two left."

"I'll take 'em. And one coffee."

She went to work filling my order. I wondered whether Huckleberry Acres was violating some child labor law. She didn't seem to mind.

"Cream and sugar are over there," she said, handing me a bag and taking my credit card.

"I'm looking for a shop to get my car window replaced," I said. "Don't suppose you know—"

"There's a garage about eight miles down the highway. Dan's Dependable Auto."

"I'm impressed. Most girls your age probably wouldn't know that."

"Why not?"

I opened my mouth, then closed it. She had me there. "I mean I didn't know that kind of stuff at your age."

"Huh," she said, and went off to wait on another customer.

Stephen strolled over and dropped his empty cup in a nearby trash can. "Something, isn't she? Even I didn't know that stuff."

I sat down at a nearby picnic table and opened my bag. "Could you go get Stuart?"

"I think he's still asleep."

"Then wake him up."

"Guys don't do that."

I sipped my coffee. "That's crazy."

"You have to know a guy really well to wake him up. You've gotta know whether he'll forgive you or go for your throat."

"Stephen, we're talking about *Stuart*. He's more likely to commit suicide than homicide."

"Fine. But don't be surprised if he hates you for making me do this."

"I'm willing to take the risk."

I bit into Donut Number One. Not bad, except for those little seeds. They always got stuck in my teeth. But tomorrow was another day—maybe lemon custard.

* * *

When we got to the garage, Dependable Dan was sitting behind the counter, streaming what looked like *Ford vs. Ferrari* on his iPad. His denim overalls were greasy and he wore a black eyepatch, making him look like a landlocked pirate.

He looked us up and down, no doubt wondering why we were in costume.

"Don't fix buggies," he said.

"Haven't got one." I pointed out the window. "Our rear windshield is bashed in. We need to replace it."

He stabbed the PAUSE icon on his tablet, sighed, and got to his feet. With his good eye he squinted at our car. "How'd that happen?"

"Long story."

He pulled a big, black binder from under the counter and leafed through it. "What's the year on that vehicle?"

I told him. He studied the book.

"Take two days to get the glass. At least."

I groaned.

"Can you get *tinted* glass for all the windows?" Stuart asked.

Dependable Dan looked up. "Why?"

"Afraid of getting—"

"Sunburned," I said.

"That'd take a week."

"Oh," Stuart said, watching the sparse traffic with disappointment.

"Have any plastic we can tape over the gap until the glass comes in?" I asked.

"Sure. Fifty bucks."

"You're kidding."

"It ain't highway robbery, if that's what you're thinking. Got expenses, you know."

I gave him my credit card. He handed me a roll of gray duct tape. "Labor's extra," he said.

I fantasized putting the tape over his other eye, but passed it to Stephen. He took the sheet of plastic and walked out the door.

After fishing a business card from my purse, I gave it to the mechanic. "Here's my phone number. Please call me as soon as the glass gets here."

We drove back to Huckleberry Acres. "Nice job on the windshield," I told Stephen. "Cuts down on the breeze."

"Probably improves the aerodynamics," he said proudly.

When we got out of the car, three families came up to us. Two kids pointed at our outfits. One looked confused; the other snickered.

I leaned toward Stephen. "Always glad to be the center of attention," I mumbled.

One of the mothers, a woman who looked grateful for something to do in this cultural black hole, bent to her son's level. "They must work here. They wear clothes to go with the campground. It's all old-fashioned."

She straightened up. "Tell us about the old days," she said excitedly.

Stephen stepped forward. "Gladly," he said, and made up something about a tribe that had lived on this land, raising bison and selling beads and ultimately dying and returning to haunt the white settlers and any others who dared to set foot here.

The little boy started to cry. His parents glared at Stephen.

Not to be outdone, Stuart started telling a more innocent story. He called it "The Golden Eagle."

But his style wasn't quite as spellbinding as usual, perhaps because he knew he could die of gunshot wounds at any moment. The children took out their cell phones and drifted away, followed by their parents.

I looked at my watch.

Only 47 hours to go.

At least.

* * *

We wandered toward the ponies.

Stephen turned to Stuart. "Sorry to wake you up this morning. Carolyn made me do it."

Stuart shrugged. "Harder and harder to get out of bed. Never know whether it's my last day on earth."

This being a very effective conversation killer, we walked on in silence.

Finally Stephen tried again. "Ever bet on the horses?"

Stuart shook his head. "Love animals too much to do that. Being a race horse must be like rowing in the galley of a slave ship. Or being whipped into building a pyramid for some Pharaoh."

The closer we got to the ponies, the worse they looked.

There were three lined up at the fence as if expecting apples or lumps of sugar.

"Man, talk about *scrawny*," Stephen said.

Frowning, Stuart stepped up to the first in line. "The roan seems to have an eye infection. I'm going to report the owner."

"You mean Mr. Huckleberry?" Stephen asked.

"Stuart, don't give your name," I said. "We're hiding. Can't trust anybody."

"Back soon," he said, and went off to make his call.

One of the other ponies, a reddish chestnut, nuzzled my hand. His eyes were so big, so sad. "Sorry," I whispered. "I got nothin'."

Turning my back on him, I leaned against the fence and scanned the horizon for suspicious cars. I seemed to be doing a lot of that lately.

A minute later Stuart was back. "Called the Humane Society animal abuse hotline. Just got a recording, but maybe they'll do something."

He moved closer. "Carolyn, I can't keep this up. Can't just keep running. Sooner or later they'll find me."

I turned to face the chestnut pony again, then scratched him between the ears. Two fat flies landed on his forehead, but I kept scratching anyway.

"We need to go on the offensive somehow, get to the Boudreauxs," I said.

Stuart gave a hollow laugh. "*Nobody* gets to those people. The old man and his daughter live in a mansion in New Orleans, a fortress protected by crooked cops. The last sucker who tried to turn on them wound up face down in a swamp."

All at once the pony reared his head and sneezed. The flies buzzed away. My hand was slimy.

"Gross," Stephen said.

I found a tissue in my purse and began to wipe. "Stuart, you're right. Maybe we should stand out by the highway with a sign that says HONK IF YOU WANT TO KILL ME. Or just call the Boudreauxs and turn ourselves in."

"Okay."

"You're not supposed to agree with me. I'm being ironic."

"Oh."

"These little ponies deserve a chance to survive, don't they? To live a normal life?"

He nodded.

"Well, so do you," I said, and tossed the tissue in a nearby pail.

* * *

That night Huckleberry Acres staged a Hot Dog and Marshmallow Roast at a campfire near the ponies. The event had been announced on a poorly photocopied flier slipped under each cabin door. And teepee flap, I guess.

About a dozen of us gathered. The kids were still on their cell phones; the parents looked hollow-eyed, desperate.

"The pony with the eye infection looks worse," I said.

"Humane Society said they'd get around to looking at them in a week or so," Stuart reported.

It was getting dark. Light from the concession stand cast shadows on the dirt. We sat in a circle on white plastic chairs around a fire pit.

The desk clerk approached with a box of hot dogs and buns. Her possible little sister carried a can of liquid fire starter and a long, green butane lighter.

A mosquito whined near my left ear. I slapped. Hurt me more than it did him.

One of the fathers stood up and pointed at Stuart. "Could you tell us another story? Or just finish the one you started?"

"A ghost story?"

The dad glanced at his little girl. "Uh, no." He sat down.

Stuart got to his feet, then paced slowly back and forth as red-braided Wendy soaked the sticks in the fire pit and they ignited with a *whump*.

"There once was a one-armed man who liked to roast hot dogs on his hook."

I looked around, hoping no one was offended. You couldn't be too careful.

Stuart looked up at the sky. I could see Venus and Orion's belt.

"People would come from miles around to see how many hot dogs he could get on his hook at once. The record was nine."

Stephen got up and started acting it out, pantomiming. Stuart looked puzzled at first, but then tried to ignore him.

The tale continued, the stakes rising to include the annual Hot Dog Eating Contest, with a prize of $10,000 or all the mustard you could eat for the rest of your life. Stephen's efforts intensified, making him look like an interpreter for the deaf who'd had three too many cocktails.

Just as the one-armed man was swallowing his 31st sausage, Stephen managed to lose his balance.

There was a gasp as he toppled into the fire, spraying sparks everywhere. He found his voice and shrieked.

I stood up and ran to the edge of the fire pit, offering my hand. Stuart did the same.

"Coming through!" yelled the young woman from the office. She was hauling a fire extinguisher. Her apparent red-haired sibling carried another canister.

With a wind-tunnel *hooooosh* and a cloud of white powder they put him out. Stuart and I helped him up, all of us coughing.

"Can't sue us," the desk clerk said. "Your fault."

The parents and kids stared.

"I'm okay," Stephen said, "except for my straw hat."

Not even an ember glowed in the pit.

"Sorry, folks," said the clerk. "Party's over. We'll keep the concession stand open for half an hour."

Stephen checked his arms for burns, but didn't seem to find any. The right hem of his pants smoked a bit. "We need more clothes," he said, and coughed once more.

I checked my watch again.

Only 42 hours left.

CHAPTER 14

IN THE MORNING I WOKE UP NOT SMELLING COFFEE.

The odor was more like burning newspaper, the unbroiled version of which had not been slipped under my door. A look in the mirror showed a fine white dust coating my face. I hoped it made me flame-repellant.

I'd slept well enough to erase the events of the previous evening, at least temporarily. That lasted about 20 seconds.

A shower got my blood moving. Reluctantly I put on my funky, smelly garments and opened the door. I'd grown over-confident, not bothering to block my path with the dresser.

The scent of lighter fluid and cremated wieners met my nostrils.

The other cabin's door flew open. "Ah," said Stephen. "I love the smell of napalm in the morning."

He looked at me. "Robert Duvall, *Apocalypse Now*. He was crazy, but not as nuts as Brando."

I felt like Martin Sheen, caught between lunatics, slowly rising from that Vietnamese swamp, dripping.

"Morning to you, too," I mumbled, and went back inside.

Taking my phone from the nightstand, I tried Gallagher again. No answer.

There was a knock at my door. "Hey," Stephen called. "Free breakfast. Leftover hot dogs and marshmallows."

"Thanks anyway."

I recalled seeing a vending machine in the office. The little red-haired girl was manning the desk when I got there.

"You look sleepy," she said.

"Must be the light." The machine was down a short hall, next to the ice. I looked in my wallet. "You have change for a five?"

She reached under the counter. "Nope. Sorry."

So I bought all the donuts they had, those little cellophane packs, one powdered and one coconut crunch. I wished they had chocolate, but you can't always get what you want.

I went back to my cabin, buying a cup of coffee on the way. The older sister acted like she didn't know me.

I asked a longer-than-usual blessing, figuring the donuts were stale. It didn't work.

After breakfast I dialed the boys next door on the room phone. Stuart answered. "Let's convene here," I said.

"Shouldn't we be talking in code or something?" he whispered.

"Don't see why. It's not wireless, and the kid at the desk doesn't seem like the type to get involved in organized crime."

"Oh."

I hung up and sat on the bed, waiting.

"Brainstorming time," I announced when we'd gathered. Stephen took the chair by the desk; Stuart couldn't quit pacing.

Stephen burped, probably from the hot dogs. He rose to his feet.

"I like the idea of going on the offensive," he said.

"Does this involve automatic weapons?" I asked. "Maybe sprinkling nails on the highway?"

He shook his head. "What kind of clown do you think I am?"

"How many kinds *are* there?"

"Listen. We park in a conspicuous but unpopulated place. We stuff one of our outfits with newspaper and rig it with a bomb. Jeremy or Nameless Girl—or both—find it, open the door, and blow themselves to kingdom come."

"Excellent. Except that would be murder, not to mention the fact that one of us wouldn't have anything to wear."

Stuart came to a halt. "Where would we get a bomb?"

"We passed a fireworks stand somewhere along the Interstate," Stephen said.

"We can't kill them with sparklers and roman candles."

"We can if we use enough of them."

"Do you know how to wire them to the ignition?"

Stephen took out his phone. "They've got everything on the Internet." He started poking.

I stood up. "Okay! Stop right there!"

"Was it something I said?" Stephen asked.

"Isn't it always? We can't make a move until we hear from Gallagher. And we especially can't make *that* one."

He shrugged and put the phone away.

We stood there for a moment. I wrinkled my nose.

"You know, we stink."

"Guess I've gotten used to it," Stephen said.

"*I* haven't," Stuart mumbled.

I picked up the room phone and dialed the front desk. Little Miss Wendy answered.

"Is there a laundry here?"

"Closed for the season. Actually, the motor on the washer burned out and they won't let me fix it."

"How about a place to buy clothes?"

"Normal ones?"

"Right."

"There's a secondhand place near Dependable Dan's."

"Thanks." I hung up.

"Stuart, we need your fashion sense."

He narrowed his eyes. "Is that because you think I'm—"

"Yeah," I said. "Because I think you and I are the only ones around here with any taste."

* * *

We ventured down the highway to a consignment shop named Sister Sue's, a place with one eerie male mannequin in the window, along with a couple of wig heads bearing hair that made Dolly Parton look like Sinead O'Connor.

There was a gravel lot in the back, where we hid the car.

The place smelled like mothballs, a distinct improvement on our musk. I went straight to the Women and Girls section; the boys got waylaid by the golf clubs and a pair of radio-controlled cars.

Sister Sue, a chubby beamer who might have been a nun if she'd had a habit, stood behind the counter and watched us warily.

Ten minutes later, she rang us up. The boys flopped an armload of clothing on the counter. Stuart added a golf club; Stephen plunked down an orange Mustang with a little wire sticking out the top. His eyes were a little too bright.

"Got any batteries?" he asked excitedly.

Sister Sue shook her head. "Try the Family Dollar down the road."

I drummed my fingernails on the counter. "Stephen, we're traveling light, remember?"

"I only got *one*."

Sighing, I laid my purchases next to theirs. Three outfits and a pair of sensible black Kizik's shoes.

We took turns getting dressed in the only fitting room. Out on the sidewalk we looked like we were roughly in the right century, though Stephen's mint-green leisure suit looked out of place. Apparently he'd rejected Stuart's advice.

Stuart looked down at his midsection. "At least I don't need a belt to hold up my pants. Didn't have any. They're at least three inches too small."

My gray wool outfit was itchy, but tasteful. I longed for my tweedy brown editor's blazer.

Down the street, at the town's only laundromat, we washed our Amishwear. We took turns standing guard, watching out the window.

When we came out, Stephen pointed next door. "Hey, look! World of Guns and Ammo! I could use a—"

"Keep walking, Texas Ranger," I said, and pushed him in the car.

* * *

That afternoon, back at the cabin, I finally got hold of Gallagher. He sounded very much alive.

"I've got to ask," I said. "How'd you get away from Jeremy and the girl?"

"Clean living," he said, and coughed. "But I've got bigger news. CNN says Max Boudreaux's dead. Natural causes, supposedly."

"Wow. We've kind of been out of the loop here."

"If you ask me, it's a power struggle. Although they always said the old man had a heart condition."

"Good news for us, right?"

He grunted. "One down and a heck of a lot more to go.

Angel's been running the show for the last few years anyway."

It hit me that I was relieved Max was dead. Was it wrong? I felt the same way about Osama Bin Laden. I'd have to consult C.S. Lewis about it someday.

"So what are *you* doing?" Gallagher asked.

"Probably better if I don't tell you where we are yet. Not exactly a secure line." I paused. "Jeremy blasted out our rear windshield. We barely got away."

"Jeez. Is it fixed?"

"Need a couple more days. We also think it might be time to go on the offensive."

"You and what army?"

"We haven't worked out the details."

"Well, that's where the devil is, lady. But I'll give it some thought."

"Thanks. Can't believe you're still standing."

"Frankly, neither can I. Let's all keep our heads down and hope Max's bucket-kicking distracts the family for a few days."

* * *

After dinner, I sat on my bed and stared at the landline. How long had it been since I'd talked to Hunter, not to mention my best friend and fellow donut enthusiast Mikki Flaherty? Did they wonder what was going on?

Hunter's curiosity, if he had any, would be strictly idle. Mikki, on the other hand, would either be sick with worry or trying speed-dating for the umpteenth time.

I picked up the phone and pressed the buttons.

All I got was her voice mail. Clearing my throat, I got ready for the beep—then hesitated.

There was no way to explain why I was one of three fugitives on the run from a family that made the Brady Bunch look like the Borgias. Not in a way that would make any sense.

The beep sounded.

"Hey, Mikki." I tried to sound perky, like Katie Couric or Kathy Gifford. "Just checking in. Things have been a little crazy around here lately; but when I get back let's get together for a whole box of you-know-whats. 'Bye."

I put the phone down. *If* I get back, I thought.

CHAPTER 15

NEXT MORNING, AT BREAKFAST, I TOLD THE BOYS ABOUT Gallagher's call.

"Max Boudreaux's dead."

Stuart smiled. "I'm devastated."

I stirred my coffee. "Gallagher's not so sure about going on the offensive. Thinks the family's nearly invincible."

"Then how'd *he* get away?" Stephen asked.

"Wouldn't tell me. Anyway, he'll think about the idea. Wants us to keep our heads down."

"Whatever that means," Stuart said.

My phone rang. Dependable Dan.

"Your glass is in. Or it will be if you get your rear end down here."

"Finally," I said.

"Hey, I warned you it would take time."

"I'll bet you've won the Angie's List award for customer satisfaction three years in a row."

"Nope. And I couldn't care less."

"We'll be there in half an hour. Until then, you might look up 'How to give a rip' on wikihow.com."

I hung up. Stephen pulled a toothpick out of his shirt pocket and started digging between his teeth.

"Who was that?"

"Not Midas or Safelite, that's for sure." I paused. "Time to say goodbye to Huckleberry Acres."

"I was just starting to like it here," Stephen said.

Stuart giggled. "Two pieces of good news in one morning. Maybe there's a God after all."

There was no formal farewell. We turned in our keys at the front desk. "Come back and see us," the older sister said. It was pretty clear she didn't mean it.

Just as we got in the car, a white van pulled up. HUMANE SOCIETY INVESTIGATIONS, it said on the side.

"Uh-oh," Stuart said. "Let's not tarry unnecessarily."

"Wish I could hear *that* conversation," I said, but headed toward the highway.

Dependable Dan took 45 minutes to install the new windshield. For a guy with one eye, he did a pretty good job. After sealing the glass with blue masking tape, he joined us in the waiting room. "Don't take the tape off for twenty-four hours," he ordered.

He presented me with the bill. One of the charges looked unfamiliar. Something about an environmental service fee.

"What's that?" I asked.

"Have to dispose of the glue properly. Hazardous waste."

"Which costs fifty dollars? What do you do, launch it into space?"

"Well, I could take the new window off if you like. Bet you can find another one down the road in a week or so."

Jaw clenched, I handed over my credit card. "Stephen, Stuart—next one's on you."

"Pleasure doing business," Dan said.

"That makes one of us."

There was a faint scent of Super Glue as we left Dan behind. Considering how much we'd paid, it seemed we should notice a more striking improvement. Like a quieter ride or more dramatic scenery.

Stephen started singing. "On the road again; just can't wait to get on the road again . . ."

"That's a miserable Willie Nelson," I said.

"It was Waylon Jennings."

"Whatever. Where do you guys think we should go next?"

"New Orleans," Stephen said.

Stuart leaned forward. "I still think getting out of the country would be best. I say Mexico."

"New Orleans would be like deliberately walking into the woods at midnight in a slasher movie. Stupid. Nothing personal."

He looked out his window. "You never like my ideas."

"Mexico would be worse. And Europe would be too expensive."

Stuart sat back. "I suppose you have the answer."

"I vote for trying to stay with Marvin Ainsley Pitts in Florida."

Stephen groaned.

"The guy who wrote *Darkness at Dawn?*" Stuart asked. "Isn't he, like, a hundred years old?"

"I know he's your friend, Carolyn," Stephen said. "But—"

"The Boudreaux family won't make a connection. And Marvin might know how to survive long enough for Gallagher to work something out."

I waited for the protests.

Sullen silence.

There being no objections, I pulled onto the shoulder, picked up my phone, and called Brother Pitts.

* * *

"Cranberry!"

That was what Marvin had called me for as long as I could remember. I was never sure why.

"Marvin," I asked, "are you sitting down?"

"Nope. Should I be?"

"Yes."

There were some rustling noises. "Okay."

"Just sit right back and you'll hear a tale, a tale of a fateful trip . . ."

"*Gilligan's Island*," he said. "Where are you, Hawaii?"

"I wish. Can't tell you our location, though. Somebody might be listening."

"You're in trouble again."

"Not just me."

I proceeded to fill him in, starting with miniature golf and ending with the windshield. I left out the part about the hot dogs.

There was a long pause. "Murder, Amish people, and the FBI. Loan sharks after you with guns. A dead mobster. And an author with a gambling problem who writes books for kids."

"That about covers it."

"So what's the problem?"

"Very funny."

"I'm well aware of the Boudreauxs. Hadn't heard about Max's demise, though."

"We can't just go home and hang Stuart out to dry."

He grunted. "You need a place to stay, is that it?"

"They'd never guess if it were *your* place."

"Just a minute."

He put his phone down. I could hear him talking it over with Tracy, his long-suffering wife. She sounded alarmed.

More conversation, mostly unintelligible. Then a pause.

"Here's my lovely bride," Marvin said. Fumbling noises.

"Carolyn?"

"So nice to hear your voice," I said, wondering whether I was finally stretching our friendship to the limit.

"You'll have to sleep on the floor in Marvin's office. And it can't be more than three weeks, because the kids are coming to visit."

"That should be more than enough."

Marvin broke in. "May I remind everyone that I have a gun?"

Tracy scoffed. "Won't do much good against the mafia or whoever this is."

"Is that a yes?"

"Only if you promise to take me to Israel when this is over."

"You've always been braver than I am," he said, trying to sound Marvin-Gaye seductive.

"And crazier, for not turning you down when you come up with stupid ideas like this." She paused. "Sorry, Carolyn."

"You're right, as usual," I said. "It's nuts."

"But nobody else has a better one. I know. We've been down this road before. The Lord's protected us so far, but there's no point in trying His patience."

I put my phone on speaker and looked at Stephen and Stuart. "Everybody say 'thank you.'"

"For what?" Stephen whispered.

"Just do it."

"*Gracias*," Stuart said.

"*Vielen Dank*," added Stephen. "Or *Danke Schoen*, if you're a Wayne Newton fan."

"Who?" Stuart asked.

"You don't want to know," I said. "Thanks, and we'll see you in a couple of days."

I hung up, started the car, took the next exit, and set a course for St. Petersburg—hoping I wasn't taking down Marvin and Tracy along with us.

* * *

Two days on the back roads were like ten on the front roads. We watched all the way for Jeremy and the Nameless Girl. The closer we got to Florida the more big, white Cadillacs we saw, driven by old people with their turn signals stuck.

Every six hours I tried to call Gallagher, except during the night. Couldn't reach him.

In Mars Bluff, South Carolina, we stopped at the Economy Inn. Stuart paid with a Visa, grumbling. "Hope the Boudreauxs don't have relatives at the credit card companies to track our purchases. And that I don't run out of money before this is over."

Next day, five miles from St. Petersburg, we came over a hill just in time to see a picture-perfect sunset. Marvin was always needling me about staying in the Big Apple, where sunsets were blocked by the buildings and nobody noticed anyway because they were all staring at their smartphones while crossing the street and getting hit by the taxi drivers.

I put on my sunglasses and turned down the visor. "Almost there," I said.

"I'd move here," said Stuart, "if I could afford plastic surgery and a fake I.D." He sighed.

When we got to the Pitts condo, Marvin answered the door.

"You can park in the carport. Got a tarp we can pull over your car."

Tracy found sleeping bags and set us up in Marvin's office. I could see fitting us all in would require more spatial intelligence than I had. Maybe Stuart's artistic eye could envision a solution. If not, Stephen could find an app for it.

Tracy started dinner and invited me into the kitchen.

"Reminds me of the Amish," I said. "The womenfolk deal with the food. The men just eat it."

"Give me a hand with the clam chowder. We usually have New England, but for you we'll try Manhattan."

I opened four cans of clams. She chopped the onions.

"Tell me more about the Amish," she said.

I did, trying not to brag about how proficient I'd gotten as a milkmaid and manure shoveler.

When I got to the part about Aaron and how he'd helped us escape, she put down her knife. "Want to see him again?" she asked.

"Oh, whatever," I lied.

Fifteen minutes later she tapped Marvin on the shoulder. "Dinner's ready."

Marvin stood. "Everybody to the table." We sat down. "Stuart," he said, "would you care to return thanks?"

Stuart blanched. But as my mother used to say, he knew which side his bread was buttered on.

"Salt is bitter, sugar is sweet. Thanks for the vittles; good God, let's eat."

When I opened my eyes, Marvin and Tracy were looking away, apparently trying not to lecture Stuart on his theology or laugh at his poetry.

"My grandma taught me that," Stuart said.

I patted his arm, knowing he'd rather be tied to the railroad tracks than pray.

Stephen was first to dig in, taking enough oyster crackers for a wading pool full of chowder.

Marvin turned to his wife. "Manhattan, is it?"

"That's right."

He nodded. "As it should be."

He turned to me and pointed at his service revolver on the buffet.

"I believe I mentioned my friend there."

"You did."

"Just in case," he whispered, and passed what was left of the crackers.

CHAPTER 16

AFTER DINNER WE SAT ON THE COUCHES. THE PITTS HAD TWO of them, at right angles—one tan, one the color of Marvin's hair. Which was slightly more gray than white.

"Let's strategize," I said.

"I love that," Stephen said. "But we usually do it with an erasable white board."

"Well, *excuse* me," Tracy said. "It's a living room, not an office."

Marvin leaned back and looked at the ceiling. "Here's what I know about the Boudreauxs. Especially Angel. Probably more ruthless than her father. Legend has it she once used a tin snips on a debtor's knuckle bones."

Stuart flinched.

"Stop!" Tracy cried, throwing a pillow at her not-so-lovely groom.

"Honey, please don't do that."

She shrugged. "Baby, it's a *throw* pillow. And this poor man doesn't need you scaring him half to death."

I leaned forward. "Here's what I don't get. If the family's

done all these things, why hasn't the FBI or whoever put them in prison?"

Marvin scratched his pointy chin. "It's like Al Capone."

"What?"

"They couldn't prove he was a mass murderer. Finally, got him on tax evasion. Maybe they could do something like that with the Boudreauxs, but the IRS seems to have better things to—"

My phone rang.

"Where *are* you?" It was Gallagher.

"We're—" I hesitated. "Call me back on the landline." I gave him the number and hung up.

Stephen lifted an eyebrow. "Gallagher?"

I nodded and moved to the other sofa, next to the lamp stand where the telephone sat. Stuart looked at his watch.

Riiiiiinnngg.

"Me again," said the gravelly voice. I put the phone on speaker.

"Have you ever heard of Marvin Ainsley Pitts?"

There was a pause. *"Darkness at Dawn?* Yeah, sure." Marvin beamed.

"We're at his place in St. Petersburg. With him and his wife."

"How'd you pull *that* off? I've followed the guy for years. Wish I could write like him, but I'm sort of dyslexic."

"He's one of a kind," I said. Marvin's grin grew wider. Tracy rolled her eyes.

"But aren't you putting them in a bad spot? You've got no protection."

Marvin waved it off. "I have a gun," he called.

"With all due respect, sir, you're outnumbered."

Marvin chuckled. "Did I mention my battalion of angels?"

Gallagher grunted. "Not my department."

Marvin winked at me.

"I'm working on finding an informant close to the family," Gallagher said. "It's not easy. The last person who infiltrated the Boudreaux mansion was a partner of mine. He ended up floating in the Gulf of Mexico."

Tracy looked at Marvin.

"Sugar, I got this," he said.

"Where have I heard *that* before?"

Gallagher cleared his throat. "Next time I'll call this number. Hope you'll be alive to answer."

* * *

Next morning, Marvin and I took an early walk on the beach. It was chilly, but the sun was just starting to clear the horizon.

"Cranberry, how you doing?"

I kicked away a piece of seaweed half-buried in the sand. "Well as can be expected."

"That's no kind of answer."

I pulled Tracy's borrowed sweater more tightly around my shoulders. "I just want to turn back the clock to the day we went miniature golfing. I'd take Stuart to the Metropolitan Museum of Art instead. After a nice afternoon of staring at Rembrandts, we'd put him on a plane back to Vermont. He might be dead by now, but at least we'd be free of the Boudreauxs."

Marvin bent down, picked up a rock with sea-bored holes in it, and tossed it away. "Makes a lot of sense, except for the time-travel part."

We resumed hiking in silence.

Marvin chose another rock and flung it into the surf. "Life's not fair, but God is good. You've done the right thing by trying to help Stuart."

A voice broke in behind us. "*Samson!*"

Marvin pulled up his sweatshirt, slipped out his revolver, and whirled around.

It was just a big dog, black, at least half Irish Wolfhound, galloping down the beach. Its little-old-lady owner, pressing her white cloche hat to her head with one hand, tried in vain to keep up.

Marvin put back the gun. Seemed an uncomfortable place to keep it, but he didn't have a purse.

"If God is so good and powerful," I said, "why carry that thing?"

He clasped his hands behind his back. "Don't tell anybody, but I never put a bullet in it. Except at the shooting range."

He looked at the ocean. The sun was higher now.

"My faith ain't in Smith and Wesson."

We watched the dog and its owner get smaller and smaller, saying nothing.

Finally, he spoke. "Powerful, yeah. But don't forget the *good* part."

* * *

Back at the condo, I helped Tracy get breakfast ready. She manhandled a heavy old waffle iron from a low kitchen cabinet and took out a steel bowl.

"My mom had one of those," I said. "Probably still does."

"Reach me the flour, would you?" she asked, and pointed to the pantry. "And the vegetable oil."

She plugged the iron into the wall. "When's the last time you had a homemade waffle?"

"Can't remember."

"Well, you're about to have a good one. Marvin sticks around mostly to get them. Lord only knows why I keep making them."

Stephen and Stuart wandered in, their hair uncombed.

"You boys get me the maple syrup."

"Where?" Stephen asked.

"I'm not tellin'. You need something to do."

Stephen opened and closed every cabinet in the room, then shook his head. "I give up."

"Try the refrigerator," Tracy said. "'Refrigerate after opening.' Means what it says."

He stuck his head in the fridge. "Wish *I* could get inside the Boudreaux mansion."

Tracy laughed. "That'd be like a sheep wanting to get inside a slaughterhouse."

He took out the bottle just as the phone on the wall rang. "Could you get that?" Tracy asked.

I picked it up.

It was Gallagher.

"Haven't found anybody to get close to the Boudreauxs, but things aren't as they seem," he said.

"How so?"

"I have reason to believe Max isn't dead after all."

CHAPTER 17

WAS IT GOOD NEWS OR NOT? I WASN'T SURE.

I put the phone on speaker.

"Listen up, everybody." All eyes went to me. "It's Gallagher."

"Okay," the voice said, and coughed. "I've had the Boudreaux place under surveillance. There's a compounding pharmacy that hand-mixes Max's heart medicine. The truck came last night."

"You watching the mansion yourself?" Stuart asked.

"Yeah. Can't afford to hire anybody. The family's announced plans for a memorial service, but nobody's seen a hearse or ambulance leave the property."

"Weird," Stephen said.

"My take is that Angel's staged a coup. Max is more or less a prisoner in his own house. If that's true, she's likely to double down to show who's in charge."

"How?" I asked.

"She'll probably call in all the IOUs from the family's clients as soon as she can track them down. Stuart's not the only one who owes big money. But you need to make him the hardest to find."

"We've covered up the car."

"I doubt that's enough."

Marvin raised his hands in a helpless gesture. "What are we supposed to do, bury it?"

"Probably not practical," Gallagher said.

Marvin rolled his eyes.

I took the phone off speaker. "We'll keep watching for the Cadillac or whatever the Nameless Girl drives."

Gallagher grunted. "No telling what they're driving now. The Boudreauxs can afford to switch vehicles every week if they want. For all I know they could both be on motorcycles."

I tried to picture Jeremy on a Harley-Davidson. Maybe he was more of a Moto Bike man.

"I'll let you know if I find a mole who can tell me what's really going on." He started coughing again.

"You back to smoking?" I asked.

"Is it that obvious?"

"Either that or you've got walking pneumonia."

"I'm down to a pack a day, alright?"

"There's a reason they call cigarettes coffin nails."

"They're still legal."

"So is saying *they* when you're talking about one person."

There was a pause. "Is that fatal?"

"So you admit tobacco's dangerous."

"Sure. But the way things are going, we may have a pretty short life expectancy anyway."

* * *

I hung up the phone. We sat there in shock.

Finally Stuart spoke. "I can't do this anymore. It's not

right to put the rest of you in jeopardy. Maybe I should just go to New Orleans and turn myself in at the Boudreauxs front gate."

"Great idea," Stephen said. "Nice knowing you."

I punched him in the shoulder.

"Ow. Quit it. You're not the boss of me."

"As a matter of fact, I am."

He looked away.

"If what Gallagher says is true, all three of us are targets," I said. "Maybe we should leave Marvin and Tracy to get them out of the line of fire."

Marvin looked at Tracy, eyebrows raised.

She shook her head. "We're in this for the duration."

"Then it's settled," I said. "We may be sitting ducks, but we don't have to take this lying down."

Tracy turned to me. "If you're gonna keep using puns like that, I'm taking back the welcome mat."

* * *

That night after dinner, we were sitting in the living room trying not to watch *Jeopardy*. Apparently, it was Marvin's favorite show and he was disgustingly good at it. He'd just wagered his imaginary $25,000 on a question about some ancient Roman senator when Stephen looked up from his phone.

"Max's memorial service is gonna be public. Live-streamed on YouTube. I think we should go."

"That's crazy," I said. The *Jeopardy* theme ticked and tocked as Marvin bit his lip.

"We could go in disguise," Stephen added.

"Why should we go at all?"

"Maybe we can plead our case to some family member. Maybe even Angel."

The Jeopardy theme faded. Marvin leaned forward, listening.

He lost everything. "That ain't fair," he growled.

Tracy picked up the remote and shut down the program. "Remember your blood pressure."

He seemed eager to reply. Then, apparently thinking better of it, he walked out.

"We'll all be in the open," Stephen continued. "Even the Boudreauxs wouldn't be dumb enough to shoot us there."

Stuart nodded. "Safer than showing up at the front gate and surrendering."

"Now, about disguises," Stephen said. "Wearing our Amish clothes would make us stand out."

"Obviously," said Stuart. "We've got regular clothes now."

"For a funeral I'd go with black suits and sunglasses."

"Have you guys got a death wish?" I asked.

"Sometimes *I* do," Stuart said.

"*I* don't. It'll be enough to watch the thing on the Internet."

Marvin came back into the room. "What did I miss?"

"Not much," Tracy said, looking relieved.

I went to the landline and called Gallagher.

"You again?"

"Are you going to Max's service?"

"No way. The family's bought half the cops and most of the politicians in town. They'll be watching for me."

"You can see it on YouTube."

He coughed once more. "Don't know how to do that stuff. How about you pay my respects for me?"

CHAPTER 18

ABOUT 10:00 A.M. THE NEXT DAY, WE STOWED THE SLEEPING bags in the closet of Marvin's office and gathered around his computer.

Marvin sat in his desk chair and pressed the power button on his aging iMac. The chime sounded, and a photo of Yosemite National Park appeared. He picked up the mouse and tried to click on Safari, but the screen was frozen.

"It does that sometimes," he said. He scrubbed the mouse back and forth on the pad, but the cursor was AWOL.

Stephen tapped him on the shoulder. "May I?"

With a grunt Marvin gave up the helm. Stephen cracked his knuckles and sat.

He tried the mouse. Nothing happened.

Standing up, he reached behind the monitor with both hands and closed one eye. "Ah. There she is."

"There *what* is?" Marvin asked.

"Disconnected. Keyboard USB from the CPU."

Tracy shook her head. "I hate these machines."

"At least it's a Mac," Stephen said, and brought up YouTube.

"We need more chairs in here," Tracy said. "Can you get some from the kitchen?"

The rest of us hauled in more seats. There was barely room to move.

Things in New Orleans were already underway. We watched as a long line of black-garbed mourners waited to get into the towering stone cathedral.

"Who's paying for this?" Stuart asked.

"The family, I guess."

They must have been paying plenty. The picture switched from exterior to sanctuary interior. At least a two-camera production, probably more.

A procession of family members made their way to the reserved seats in front. The pipe organ was doleful. There was Angel, a couple of young men, a few kids, and two older women. Their names flashed on the screen.

"Anybody see Jeremy?" I asked. "Or the girl?"

I waited. Nobody said "I do," which I took as a no.

Angel, all in black, had a veil over her face. I couldn't remember the last time I saw one of those.

"Hmm," said Marvin. "Closed casket."

"Something unusual about that?" Stuart asked.

"He supposedly died of a heart attack, not a car accident. Presumably they could make him presentable. I'd expect folks like that to file past, look in, give the sign of the cross, that sort of thing."

A short, gray-haired priest, in a black chasuble trimmed with silver, mounted the platform and stood behind the podium. He recited something in Latin, my grasp of which is limited to phrases like *quid pro quo* and *illegitimus non carborundum*, the meaning of which is widely disputed.

Next came two little girls, not twins but garbed alike in daffodil-yellow dresses and white gloves. They did their best to sing *Ave Maria*, a hymn that would challenge Pavarotti.

They must have been close friends of the family, because they never would have made it past the first round on *America's Got Talent*.

Tracy groaned. "Can you turn the sound down?"

Stephen punched the volume key a few times. It made a series of fading *boings*.

That served us well in what followed. The eulogies were endless. At least four men waxed poetic about what a great humanitarian and father Max had been.

Marvin sighed through most of it, shaking his head at the undeserved plaudits.

After the men came the head of the city council, according to the title on the lower left of the screen. She was African-American, a woman I remembered excoriating the White House during Hurricane Katrina. In tones that soared up and down like those of a National Baptist preacher, she recounted the time Max donated money to rebuild the Lower Ninth Ward.

Finally the priest delivered a homily about the rich man who kept building bigger and bigger barns to hold all his wealth, only to lose it when he died. I couldn't tell whether he was praising Max or delivering a well-disguised jab. I doubted even he could get away with the latter.

Stephen leaned toward me. "I can't figure out all the chanting and kneeling and standing," he whispered.

"In the first place, it's not chanting. It's responsive reading. In the second place, you're not there. You can keep sitting."

The priest switched from Latin to English. "Private interment will follow the reception." Back to Latin, he lifted his hand and did what appeared to be blessing the congregation.

It made me glad I wasn't Catholic. Worship was a lot of work. In my church, all you really had to know was where to buy coffee in the foyer.

The organ played something medieval as the family left the front benches, half to one exit and half to the other. The pews slowly emptied.

Marvin sat back in his chair. "Luke, chapter twelve: 'You fool, tonight your soul is required of you. The things you've prepared—whose will they be?' Not an exact quote, but close enough."

He scratched his chin. "That's what happens when you lay up treasure for yourself and aren't rich toward God."

"Amen," Tracy said.

* * *

Stephen was about to shut down the computer when the scene changed again.

"Must be the reception," I said. I wondered whether cathedrals had basements.

There were no titles this time as Angel greeted guests in the reception line. Her veil was gone.

The embraces were warm, but the look in her eyes was cold. She was guarded on both sides by black-suited gentlemen with large muscles.

Suddenly there was a flash, like a picture being taken. The guards moved to shield her.

A chubby, middle-aged man in a rumpled brown suit, maybe paparazzi, lowered his smartphone. He looked surprised when the guards spirited him away.

"Wouldn't want to be that guy," Stephen said.

Everyone on the screen acted like nothing had happened. One guard returned.

Angel got back to the work of grieving. Some of the relatives left. There remained only two—a stone-faced young man and an elderly woman who looked like she'd spent a lifetime denying the obvious.

The picture froze. "Kernel panic," Stephen said. "I can't thaw it."

He switched off the machine and turned to Marvin. "Don't worry, it'll come back when you restart. Probably."

"Wonder what happened to the photographer," Stuart said. Nobody wanted to speculate.

I stared at the dead screen. "Nice to finally see the person who most wants to kill you."

Maybe *nice* wasn't the right word.

Maybe *terrible* was a better one.

* * *

Stephen seemed unperturbed.

"Seeing the refreshments made me hungry," he said.

Tracy closed her eyes. "Peanut butter's in the pantry. Jelly's in the fridge."

"Oh," he said, crestfallen. Probably disappointed she wasn't whipping up a full-fledged brunch.

I went to the window. A gray day, but the air conditioning's roar told me it was hot as ever.

"Still not used to the palm trees and waves," I said to nobody in particular. "But I'd like the chance to if I ever got to retire, which I—"

"Look," squeaked Stuart.

He directed my gaze to the parking lot, where a car was pulling in.

White Cadillac. New.

I tensed as two people climbed out.

Not the two I was thinking of. An older couple in Hawaiian print shirts and floppy hats.

"Whew," Stuart said.

I was about to take my chair back to the kitchen when another car arrived, parking at the edge of the lot.

A gray Jeep Wrangler. It sat there a full minute.

At last two figures emerged. One was Jeremy, his arm in a sling.

The other was the Nameless Girl. Both wore sweatshirts and jeans.

I swallowed and faced the others.

"We have visitors," I said.

CHAPTER 19

"Where's the best place to hide in this complex?" I asked, wishing I'd done so before.

Marvin and Tracy looked at each other.

"Laundry room, probably," she said. "Hardly anybody goes there anymore. Three bucks to wash, three to dry. Most folks use a laundry service. For twenty-eight dollars a month they pick up your stuff, clean and fold it, then deliver it right to your—"

Marvin patted her on the shoulder. "I think they get it," he said, and dashed into the hallway.

The rest of us followed. After pausing to lock the condo, he led us to the elevator. A handmade sign about TACO TUESDAY, 7 P.M. was taped next to the door, along with a photo of a missing chihuahua named General Douglas MacArthur.

The car was crowded. I hoped nobody could hear my heart pounding.

"First floor," he said, and pressed the button.

When the door slid open, we all retreated a step. But the hall was empty.

The laundry room smelled like mold and chlorine. No lock on the door. No chairs. A jumbo bottle of Tide sat on the washer.

Stephen looked at the floor, then bent down. "Hey, free sock!" he said, holding up a puffy purple orphan covered with what looked like cat hair. After displaying it like a trophy, he tossed it in a pail under the change machine.

"Please use your inside voice," I whispered.

"Yes, Ma'am."

We waited, listening.

Finding a towel on the floor, I stuffed it under the door. My second college roommate had used that trick to keep narcs from smelling her marijuana smoke. Maybe it would block sound waves, too.

Marvin and Tracy, looking tired, sat on the washer and dryer respectively. "There's a lock on the door," he said. "Could you push that button?"

Stuart reached out and did so, his finger trembling.

Suddenly we heard running footsteps from the floor above. Apparently, Jeremy and the Nameless Girl had started at the top and were working their way down. Or some senior marathoner was practicing for the next Iron Person competition.

Tracy turned to her husband. "What did you say about the IRS?" she whispered.

For a moment he seemed confused. "Oh," he said finally. "They got Al Capone for tax evasion."

Tracy turned my way and kept her voice down. "Used to be a bookkeeper. *I* never did this, of course, but crooks tend to keep two sets of books. One for the government, one with real numbers. If we could get the real one—"

Marvin shook his head. "Baby, that's a job for Mr. Gallagher's informant—*if* he ever finds one."

We listened again. Two sets of feet pounded down our hallway.

I held my breath. The galloping racket passed.

Steps faded down the stairs. Then nothing.

Nobody spoke for at least a minute.

Until Stephen did.

"That *can't* be it," he said. "Too easy."

* * *

I pulled the towel from beneath the door and strained to hear. A dog barked from somewhere. General MacArthur, perhaps.

Then came a huge THUMP and the sound of a doorframe cracking. "Uh-oh," Marvin said. "Sounds like our place."

Tracy shut her eyes. "They'll trash it."

"Better without us there."

There was crashing and banging.

"Searching the cabinets," Marvin said.

"For what?" Stuart asked.

I backed away from the door. "Us. Or money. Or both."

After a few minutes the sounds subsided.

But the wail of a siren replaced them.

"Got a silent alarm," Marvin explained. "First time it's gone off."

A door slammed.

I tossed the towel back on the floor. "Let's take a look."

They trailed me to the nearest window, at the end of the hall. We looked down on the parking lot.

The Wrangler pulled out, just seconds before a squad car rolled in.

* * *

"Man, what a mess."

The officer, a young man with a valiant attempt at a mustache, took off his cap and wiped his forehead with it.

His partner, a slightly older pony-tailed woman who seemed unfazed by the heat, picked up a sofa pillow and threw it back on the couch. "Who's the homeowner?" she asked.

Marvin and Tracy raised their hands.

"Want to file a report?"

"Are you kidding? Of *course* I do," Marvin said. "This may be low priority for you, but it's high for me."

Tracy sighed and patted his back. "Baby, it's just *stuff*."

He looked at me for support, then deflated. "Yeah, *my* stuff."

I wondered whether to tell the cops the whole story. This was no run-of-the-mill breaking-and-entering, though they undoubtedly assumed it was.

They'd never believe me. Not to mention the others.

The fuzzy-lipped cop handed Marvin a form. "Fill this out. I'd advise you to get the door fixed as soon as you can. Change the locks, too."

Marvin turned to me. "Yeah, I know. 'Don't forget the *good* part.'"

CHAPTER 20

THE CONDO MAINTENANCE MAN TOOK HALF AN HOUR TO SHOW up. He must have been at least 80, with a teal Miami Dolphins cap and a leather belt so stuffed with tools he looked like a suicide bomber.

"You got a problem with the door?"

Marvin pointed at the doorframe, which was splintered on the lock side. "Think you can shore it up?"

"What'd you do, try to get a piano in here?"

"You might put it that way."

He pulled out a crowbar. "Take me about fifteen minutes, tops."

Marvin leaned toward me. "More like an hour. We'll be lucky if we can open it when he's done."

We sat around and watched as the old man undid the brass hinges, whacked the frame until it was more or less square, and kept trying to get the door to swing. He took a sheet of sandpaper from the pocket of his overalls, ground away the splinters, and smoothed the threshold. Stephen ignored the home repair lesson and watched what sounded like Jimmy Kimmel on his smartphone.

After replacing the hinges, the repairman patted the door as if it were a favorite horse.

Marvin checked his watch. "I stand corrected. Forty-five minutes."

Tracy cleared her throat. "Marvin, give the man a tip."

"Baby, the condo association pays his—"

"Do unto others."

He grunted and took a $20 bill from his wallet. "Hasn't even gotten to the lock yet."

"He will."

After taking the money, the old man touched the brim of his cap. "Back in the morning."

"*Morning?*" Marvin cried. "We could be *dead* by then."

"From moving another piano?"

"Natural causes," Marvin said.

"Tell you what. If you're dead in the morning, you don't have to tip me again." He picked up his hammer and pulled the door shut behind him. Took three attempts to close it all the way.

Tracy turned to me. "It keeps him busy. I think he's the manager's father."

She looked around and shook her head. "Anyone care to help me pick this place up?"

Stuart raised his hand. Stephen was too absorbed in YouTube to notice.

"Off to the bathroom," Marvin said. "At my age, you can't be too careful."

I figured it was time to call Gallagher again—on the landline, of course.

He let loose with a four-letter Anglo-Saxonism when he heard what had happened. "Pardon my French," he added, not sounding the least bit contrite.

"It's not French," I said, "but never mind."

"I'll get there as soon as I can. You can't stay. The good

news is I've found somebody who might be able to help us on the inside."

"Who?"

"At this point, better you don't know. For your sake and his."

"Tracy's got an idea. You know how crooked accountants keep two books, one that's secret and a doctored one for the tax people?"

"Yeah, why?"

"Don't you think that's what the Boudreauxs do?"

"I'm only ninety-nine percent sure. But they're probably in a safe at the mansion. Or some sleazy lawyer's office. Getting access would be like breaking into the White House. I'll see what I can do."

* * *

When everything was back in place, we were all hungry. But nobody felt like cooking.

"Let's do pizza," Stephen said.

Tracy and Stuart shrugged. I didn't bother to vote.

We let Marvin pick the toppings. It was his place, after all.

While we waited for the delivery person, we talked about our next move.

"We'll stay put," Tracy said. "If y'all are gone, the Boudreaux family won't have any reason to be interested in us." Marvin nodded.

"Always wanted to live on a houseboat," Stephen declared. "You know, like James Garner did on *The Rockford Files*."

"That was a trailer. On the beach, not the water."

"Then who was the guy with the houseboat?"

I thought for a moment. "Travis McGee. But I don't know anybody who lives in a houseboat, do you?"

"Not in real life."

I looked at Stuart.

"Are you *sure* you can't scrape together the money you owe, or at least most of it?"

"How?"

"Maybe take out a *real* loan against your house or something."

He shook his head. "Already have a second mortgage."

The doorbell rang. I jumped.

"Calm down, Cranberry," Marvin said. "Probably just our dinner."

It was, borne by an unarmed young woman with braces on her teeth. I tipped her, Marvin having suffered enough for one day.

Tracy got out paper plates and a six-pack of Dr. Pepper, then asked the blessing.

We chewed in silence.

Suddenly Marvin sat up straight.

"Mercy," he said.

"What?" I asked.

"Got an idea," he said.

* * *

"We can raise the money," he continued. "In a manner of speaking."

I took a bite with a slice of pepperoni on it. "We're listening."

"Years ago I met a guy in Kansas. Almost wrote a book about him. He'd been a counterfeiter, one of the best."

We waited as he gulped some Dr. Pepper and stifled a burp.

"Name was Albert Treacher. He'd done twenty years in a federal prison. Must be 70 by now. A true artist, if you overlook the illegality of the thing."

Tracy shook her head.

"The man was proud of his craftsmanship, but didn't want to call attention to himself by doing a book."

"I don't see how that could work," I said. "For one thing, the family will recognize counterfeit money."

"Eventually, sure. But if we can raise enough *real* money to cover the fake bills in a briefcase, we might be able to buy enough time for Gallagher's plan to work. Or for the IRS to get off its backside." He took another bite.

"Wouldn't they have confiscated his plates?"

"Before I left, Albert told me a secret. Not sure why. He'd hidden one set of fifties, but never told me where."

I leaned back in my chair. This dinner was giving me gas.

"Does Albert have his own printing press?" I asked.

"Probably not. But that's your department. You're in publishing. Got contacts, right?"

"Not with anybody who prints money in his *basement*."

"All we need is somebody who's . . . flexible."

"Marvin, I can't believe you're proposing doing something so wrong."

"We're not going to *spend* it, just use it as a prop. We can promise that in writing."

I groaned. "Where does Mr. Treacher live?"

"Just a minute." He went into his office.

"Anybody need another drink?" Tracy asked. Nobody responded.

A few moments later, Marvin returned with a scrap of paper. "Found this in my file. Old address in Kansas."

Stephen put both hands on his kneecaps, as if eager to get started. "Well, at least we know where to go next."

I picked up my last bit of cold pizza and chewed it, staring blankly at the wall.

CHAPTER 21

BEING TOO TIRED TO DRIVE TO KANSAS MYSELF, I THREW caution to the winds and let Stephen and Stuart take turns. We stopped only for coffee, snacks, and the bathroom breaks those activities made essential.

When the two boys were awake, they sang "Seventy-six Trombones" over and over until I literally screamed. Our destination was River City, a little sun-baked town in Kansas. My two Music Men kept chanting, "We got trouble, trouble, trouble, right here in—"

"*Shut. Up.*"

They'd snicker and call me Carolyn the Librarian, then eat their Funyuns and Slim Jims and pass out.

At about ten o'clock the next morning we checked into the town's only motel, which the sign dubbed MOTEL.

"Mmm," said Stuart, stretching. "Very creative."

I drove around the back and hid the car.

Stephen yawned. "Can we get breakfast? I'm out of Funyuns."

"There's a Carl's Jr. down the street," I said.

"Great. They're the sloppiest. Love their commercials."

"I hate 'em." I paused. "We'll walk. Don't want to move the car."

Never mind what we ordered. It was salty, messy, had a stupid name, and cost too much.

Passing one cornfield after another, we drove to Treacher's old address on the edge of town. I spotted the mailbox, but couldn't see much else.

"Oh, man!" Stephen said. "An earth house!"

I took another look. All I saw was a lump in the dry ground, a swelling no higher than I was tall. With a door. It looked like something J.R.R. Tolkien might have built for a homeless Hobbit.

I didn't see a vehicle. "Maybe it's abandoned," Stuart said.

I got out and leaned on the hood of our car. The Music Men followed.

Suddenly an old man in a tan suede vest and baggy jeans stepped out the door with a rifle. His ponytail was steel gray.

"Wow," Stephen said. "I wouldn't expect someone that eco-conscious to carry a gun."

I raised my hands. The two boys did the same.

"Albert Treacher?" I asked.

He narrowed his eyes. "Maybe."

"Marvin Ainsley Pitts sent us."

"You lie."

I shook my head. "Told us all about you. Mostly that you're the best at what you do."

He grunted. "*Used* to do."

"We've got a business proposition for you."

He raised an eyebrow and lowered his weapon. "Marvin, eh?"

"Can we come inside?"

Still looking skeptical, he nodded. "Only if you're not packing."

"As in 'packing heat'?" I asked.

"Or wired."

"No guns, no wires."

"You got five minutes," he said, and waved us inside.

* * *

Albert didn't offer us anything, but leaned his rifle against an ancient stereo. An old LP by Herb Alpert and the Tijuana Brass lay on top. The one with a half-nude girl enveloped in whipped cream, or so it would appear. There was a rose-shaped blob on her hair.

Stephen stared. *"Whipped Cream & Other Delights.* A classic."

I folded my arms. "My uncle used to have that album. If you look closely, you'll see she's really wrapped in cotton or something. And it's shaving cream, not Redi-Whip. Cheaper. But don't look closer. Raging hormones could affect your judgment."

"Take a load off," Albert said, and nodded toward a sagging charcoal couch that may or may not have seen better days. We all sat.

"Marvin said you hid your favorite counterfeiting plates," I began.

"Heck, you don't spend a lot of time on niceties, do you?"

"We don't have a lot of time."

"Why not?"

I explained our predicament. He maintained a bemused expression, as if he couldn't believe such amateurs had managed to survive despite themselves.

"And you want me to print you up some nice new money."

"No, just sell us the plates."

He laughed.

"Where are they?"

He shrugged. "Can't remember."

We looked at each other.

"Do you have a general *idea?*" Stuart asked.

"In a cornfield, I think. Down the road apiece, but I couldn't tell you *what* road or how far a piece."

Stuart sighed.

"Didn't make a map," the old man continued. "Never could draw worth anything."

Stuart scratched his chin. "We could start looking when the sun goes down. Too hot now."

"Also, we don't know whether the white Cadillac followed us," I said. "How many cornfields are there around here?"

Albert thought for a moment. "Six, maybe seven. All look alike to me."

"What did you bury the plates in?"

"Big old steamer trunk."

Stephen snapped his fingers. "We could use a metal detector."

The old man leaned back and laced his fingers behind his head. "These plates are steel, which means they'd set off a detector. Too bad we don't have one. Don't know anyone who does. Besides, the wooden box they're in is too thick."

Closing his eyes, he put the back of his hand to his forehead. "Now, wait a minute. Seems the field I used had a windmill next to it. Could narrow it down."

We waited for more. Nothing came.

I checked my watch.

"Am I the only one who's hungry?" Stephen asked.

Albert opened his eyes. "Hit a deer on the highway last week and put it in the freezer."

Stephen gasped. For a guy who loved hamburgers, he was remarkably sensitive to a short list of animals with big, brown eyes.

"I could whip up an omelet or something," Stuart suggested.

Albert frowned. "What's in all this for me?"

"You can have half the cash we're going to raise," I said, "plus the joy of doing what you do best. After all, why keep the plates all this time unless you hoped to use them again?"

With a grunt, Albert got up, fished in the freezer, and found half a dozen dinners. Probably freezer-burned. Better than eating Bambi's dad, though.

"Okay if I play this record?" Stephen asked as the old man turned on the oven.

"Suit yourself."

Stephen lifted the hi-fi's lid and put the platter on the turntable. "A Taste of Honey" blared from the antique speakers.

Twenty minutes later, we all sat in the living room, gnawing chicken legs so gnarly they could have been severed from Foghorn Leghorn. The only way I could tell the mashed potatoes from the corn was by color.

"They don't make 'em like this anymore," Albert said, smacking his lips.

"Thank God," Stuart said, sawing at a chunk of meat with a butter knife.

"Sorry the TV's busted," muttered the old man.

I looked out the front window, watching for *trouble, trouble, trouble* in you-know-where.

* * *

The sun had set by the time we'd all picked the sinews from our teeth. We squeezed into the car and started looking for cornfields.

"Reminds me of that Stephen King movie," Stuart said. "*Children of the Corn.* Don't know where that man gets his idea, but you'll never find Jennifer Jenner murdering hapless travelers."

"A windmill," I said, pulling over.

"Corn's high as an elephant's eye," Stephen said.

"*Oklahoma!*" said Stuart. "Now *there's* a drama worthy of your time."

I parked at the edge of the field, as far from the farmhouse as possible.

Albert had scrounged up three prehistoric flashlights, a couple of shovels, a hoe, and a big stick. We got out of the car and I divvied them up.

"How deep did you bury the trunk?" I asked.

"Not very. Don't care much for manual labor. But I remember dragging it to the middle of the field and hiding it there."

"Let's do this like on TV," Stephen said, "when they fan out at arms' length and search for a dead body. Except they have dogs, which wouldn't help here."

"There are only four of us," I said. "So it'll take longer. Just move slowly down the rows, sticking your shovel or whatever in the ground every yard or so."

We switched on the flashlights. At least the batteries were working.

It got darker and darker. We kept hitting rocks.

After two hours or so, the flashlights were fading. We'd found four boulders and the bones of what I hoped was an errant cow.

"I give up," Stephen said.

I sighed. "Guess we should turn back and—"

With a scraping sound my shovel hit something hard. My heart rate sped up.

"Found something."

Albert and I held the flashlight while the boys got to work.

Stuart was the first to hit wood.

"I think it's the trunk," he said, panting.

We all pried the box from the ground. The smell of wet dirt was everywhere. A huge, rusty lock held the hasp.

"Don't have the key anymore," Albert said.

"No problem," Stephen said, and lunged at the lock with his shovel, snapping it off.

The plates were inside, wrapped in clear plastic.

"Mission accomplished," said Stephen.

There was a rumbling sound, then a wet *hissssss*.

I gasped as a sheet of cold water hit me in the side of the head.

"Oh, crap," Albert said. "Irrigation system."

Stephen and Stuart grabbed the handles on the side of the trunk and began dragging it away.

Already soaked, I shivered and gathered up the tools.

"Put it in the car," I called.

A chorus of thumps and clanks came from the trunk as we unloaded our treasures.

My hair was a mess, my hands muddy.

Turning the key in the ignition, I headed for Albert's place.

CHAPTER 22

DRIPPING WET, I WATCHED AS STEPHEN AND STUART LOWERED the trunk onto the living room floor. The mud was an almost perfect match for Albert's carpet.

I wanted to change my clothes and grab a hair dryer, but that would have to wait.

Stephen lifted the lid. "Man, that *smell*," cried. "Did something die in here, or what?"

"Probably," Albert said. "Could be a mole, maybe a prairie dog."

"In that case, you can unwrap the plates yourself."

"Be glad to," the old man said proudly. "Been a long time."

The plastic was wet. Gingerly Albert peeled it off, then wiped his hands on his pants.

He held up the plates, one in each hand. I stepped closer to get a better look.

"Anybody got a fifty?" I asked. "A real one, I mean."

Nobody did, of course.

The plates looked authentic, but I was no numismatist. All I knew was that the image of Ulysses S. Grant was backward. Which it was supposed to be.

Stephen washed his hands in the sink, then took out his phone. A minute or so of Web surfing left him paler than usual.

"Oh, cripes. Did you know having counterfeit money is Criminal Possession of a Forged Instrument in the First Degree, which is also a class C felony?"

Albert grinned. "Just part of the fun."

"Says you. And I quote: 'You are guilty of this offense if you knowingly present counterfeit currency to another person in a fraudulent attempt to acquire goods or services with it.'"

"Which is exactly what we're going to do," I said.

"Extenuating circumstances," Stuart declared. "Self-defense. A matter of life and death."

Albert set the plates on the couch. "How you gonna get the money printed? Ain't no offset presses within 200 miles."

"That's Carolyn's job," Stephen said.

The old man shook his head. "You know any printers smart enough to pull this off but dumb enough to actually do it?"

I thought for a moment.

"Yeah, I do. Been almost twenty years since I did a press check at Ottoman Lithographics in Tennessee. Wonder whether they're still in business."

If what I'd read a couple of years ago in *Publishers Weekly* was true, they'd be perfect.

Unfortunately.

* * *

Next day at noon a hastily arranged flight brought me to Nashville International Airport. As we descended I could see the Parthenon. Not the Greek one, just a concrete replica in a downtown park.

Ottoman Lithographics was a red-brick former warehouse high as Hoover Dam and wide as a city block, in a part of town where no sane person would venture at night without a whole crate of pepper spray.

It was pretty much as I remembered, only grimier, and the memories it brought back made me shudder.

I'd come here alone to check the colors and registration of Stuart's second children's book, *The Very Hangry Blue Gorilla*. The cigar-smoking, union-protected, bullet-headed foreman had treated me as if I were a neophyte, which I was. When I questioned whether there was too much magenta on the simian's cheeks, he'd removed the cigar from his mouth and snorted.

"Cost five thousand big ones to make a change at this stage."

I'd held my ground for a good 60 seconds.

I hoped he was dead by now.

In the old days, Ottoman was known mainly for two things: producing half the Midwest's phone books on its massive web presses, which had been lowered through the roof by a helicopter—and printing a soft-core, now-defunct porn magazine called *Duke*.

Climbing the front steps now, I noticed the parking lot was half empty. The magazine market had withered, and hardly anybody used phone books anymore. Maybe they'd be desperate enough to take on a job that could earn the ire of the Secret Service and land them all in prison.

There was no receptionist. I found the front office and asked the drowsy secretary, a woman doing a crossword puzzle, who to talk to about a major print job.

She put down her pencil. "Major? Really?"

"Has to be done right."

For a moment she looked worried, then seemed to

remind herself she'd have to exude confidence if she wanted her next paycheck.

She picked up the phone, called somebody and pointed to the inner door.

"In there's your man. Jimmy Irving."

I thanked her, went inside, and discovered Mr. Bullet Head had moved to management. Still smoking cigars, though, with his sleeves rolled up.

A spark of recognition seemed to go off in his brain, then faded. He tapped the ashes from his cigar in a glazed pottery topless mermaid dish.

"Help you?" he asked, grinning a grin that revealed one gold tooth.

"I need you to do something impossible."

"Uh-huh. Well, the difficult we do immediately. The impossible takes a little longer."

I'd seen that somewhere before. I think it was in *Unbearable Cliché* magazine.

"I made that up," he added.

"No you didn't."

He looked out the window. "Take a seat and enlighten me."

* * *

I sat across from him. "Are we being recorded?"

He raised an eyebrow. "*Now* you got my interest."

I explained the situation, starting with miniature golf but leaving out Stuart's name, the word *Boudreaux*, and the Amish parts. Also the stories about using tin snips on people's knuckle bones and the scary legal stuff Stephen had found online.

"We only need to print enough counterfeit money to fill a briefcase. And only temporarily. I'd be willing to sign something saying it's all my fault, that your company had no intent to defraud anyone."

He tapped more ashes from his cigar. "How much you willing to pay?"

Trying to sound casual, I named a figure.

He chuckled.

I named another.

He shook his head.

"I could throw in a freezer full of venison," I offered.

He took the cigar from his mouth and looked at me as if I were crazy, possibly dangerous.

"And I promise not to do a press check."

He lifted his chin. His eyes narrowed.

"Wait a minute. I remember you."

I swallowed.

"What was it, twenty years ago?"

"In that neighborhood."

He took a puff of the cigar. "Our lawyer's been . . . incarcerated temporarily due to a little misunderstanding. Think you can draw up the paperwork?"

I nodded.

"Good. How long has that deer been in the icebox?"

"It's practically fresh."

I wasn't sure the USDA would agree. But I was an editor, not a meat inspector.

"Then we got a deal," he said, and winked.

CHAPTER 23

I was back at the motel by suppertime and picked up Stephen and Stuart.

"How'd it go?" Stephen asked.

"They went for it. Going to cost us, though."

Stuart wrung his hands. "How much?"

"I'll explain later."

When I got to Albert's underground paradise, he greeted us at the door.

"Hope you brought your appetite. I'm about to thaw dinner."

I shuddered. "Not more chicken legs."

He shook his head. "Velma."

I stared. Shades of Hannibal Lecter.

"Who's Velma?"

He motioned us toward the couch. "That's what I named the buck."

"Thank God," I said. "For a minute I thought—"

Then I remembered. "Stop!"

"How come?"

"Had to give up the venison to sweeten the deal. Cash and dead deer for a print run."

Albert frowned.

"Glad to hear I don't have to eat it," Stephen said. "But that's not exactly a freezer full of venison."

I told him how much I'd promised to pay.

"That's a bargain."

Albert sighed. "I got canned chili. Don't think it's expired yet." He headed for the kitchen.

We sat down. "I have to draw up some paperwork. To keep Ottoman Lithographics smelling like a rose."

Albert yelled from the kitchen. "How green should chili be?"

Stuart put his fist to his mouth as if it might calm his stomach.

I picked up Albert's landline. "Stephen, you remember the woman in Legal who helped when I was in jail? Flew all the way to Seattle in the middle of the night."

Stuart lowered his hand. "You were in jail?"

"Don't ask," I said.

Stephen nodded. "Gina Casebeer."

"Thought I'd get her advice."

A tired voice answered. She always sounded exhausted. Or maybe it was only when she heard from me.

"This is Carolyn Neville."

There was a long pause. "Oh," she said flatly.

"I know it's two hours later in New York."

"But you seem to have called anyway."

"I've got a legal problem."

"Are you incarcerated?"

"Not yet."

She sighed. "I've been running myself ragged leading a two-day copyright seminar—trying to explain concepts that your boss, Mr. Thicke, can't seem to understand."

"I'll get right to the point. I need to get some counterfeit money printed to save the life of one of our authors who's in debt to a loan shark." Clearly demented, even for me.

Silence.

"The company that's going to do it needs a letter exonerating them."

Remarkably, more silence.

"Ms. Neville, if I assist in any way, I'll lose my license to practice law. I suggest you all turn yourselves in to the police or FBI and give the plates to the Secret Service."

"So you're . . . reluctant."

"And you're perceptive. The best I can do is pretend we never had this conversation."

No point in arguing. "Thanks," I said, and hung up.

Couldn't afford to burn that bridge. Unless I died or she quit, we'd probably run into each other again.

"Success?" Stephen asked.

"Not exactly. She's got too much sense for my own good."

I got on the Internet and found one of those sites that helps you write your canned last will and testament. Not surprisingly, there were no forms for disclaimers absolving others of felonies.

I scratched my chin. The last novel I'd edited for Harrison Yoder had a written confession in it. It was the closest thing I could think of.

On Amazon I downloaded the e-book and found the right page, then put my phone away.

"Dinner is served," Albert yelled from the kitchen.

Stuart blanched.

Stephen leaned forward. "I vote for take-out," he whispered.

Albert appeared in the doorway, wiping his hands on a none-too-clean dish towel.

"Something's come up," I said.

Stuart put his hand to his lips again.

"Back in the morning," I said.

Albert shrugged. "All the more for me."

We picked up Burger King on the way back to the motel, then split up to our rooms.

With a Whopper in one hand and my phone in the other, I used Harrison's passage as a model. The more I reread it, the more preposterous it sounded.

Finally I printed it out on the motel's inkjet.

It ran out of ink on the last word, *document*, which I added in pencil.

* * *

Next morning, back at Albert's, I was surprised he hadn't succumbed to food poisoning.

I read my Magna Carta to the group.

Albert wagged a finger. "Can't promise not to do a press check. Took me almost a year to engrave those plates. This is like xeroxing the Mona Lisa."

"You don't have to sign it." I nodded toward Stephen and Stuart. "Neither do you."

I made no corrections since the printer didn't work, and signed on the bottom line.

Before we left, I picked up Albert's phone. Seemed like a good time to check in with Gallagher.

He was there. I could tell from the coughing.

I told him about all the progress we'd made.

"Insane," he said.

"True, but—"

"The circumstances probably would keep you out of prison, but the boys in the Secret Service don't have much of a sense of humor."

"It only has to work long enough for your informant to get the second set of books."

"Can't guarantee that'll ever happen. Can't guarantee your safety, either, if you show up at the Boudreaux mansion with that briefcase."

* * *

Next day I ferried the plates to Ottoman Lithographics. I kept them in one of Albert's empty cartons of two dozen frozen dinners on the empty seat next to me, wishing I could handcuff it to my wrist. I'd checked the suitcase full of dead deer packed with dry ice.

When I got to the front office, Jimmy the Bullet Head looked up from the latest issue of *Maxim* and smiled. There was no cigar in his mouth, but the place smelled like a tire fire.

"Whatcha got for me?"

I handed him the letter. "Your protection."

He read it silently, his fat lips moving, then set it on his desk. "I'm going out on a limb, you know."

"Not as far as *I* am."

"When do I get the venison?"

I pointed at my suitcase. "Brought it with me."

He stood. "Hey," he yelled to his secretary. "Stuff as much as you can of this meat in the lunchroom freezer. I'll take it home later."

He picked up his phone. "I'll get Carl Pinkerton. Press foreman."

Five minutes later a sixtyish guy in a tan jumpsuit and ink-spattered painter's cap limped in, hands in his pockets.

"This here's our client," Jimmy said, jerking a thumb in my direction. Carl nodded, his gaze lingering.

"Don't I know you?"

"Hope not."

He shrugged.

Jimmy sat on the edge of his desk. "Carl, gotta swear you to secrecy."

"Okay."

He turned to me. "Where's the plates?"

I held up the carton.

He took the box and unwrapped them, held them up to the light, then whistled.

"I don't know much about art, but I know what I like."

"You made that up, too, I bet."

He passed the plates to Carl. Careful to touch them only on the edges, he pulled a pair of reading glasses from his pocket and brought Albert's masterpieces closer.

"Don't know much about counterfeiting, but I know good workmanship. This is pretty amazing."

"You can't tell anybody," his boss warned.

"I said okay, didn't I?" He put the glasses away. "Just one problem."

Jimmy frowned. "What?"

He set the plates back on the desk. "Gonna be hard enough to match the inks. But finding paper with the right rag content and colored fibers will be like finding a unicorn."

"Do the best you can."

Carl took off his cap and tapped the brim on the desk. "Seems to me there's a small stash of the stock we used twenty years ago when we did wedding announcements for George Ottoman's granddaughter. Not an exact match, but maybe close enough."

"Then let's get going." Jimmy picked up a cigar and bit off the tip. "I mean you two get going. I'd just get in the way." Glancing at his magazine, he sat down.

The press room was cavernous. The ink smelled like

blueberries and solvent. A hint of machine oil hung in the air.

The press was the size of a dinosaur, black and yellow. There was a clacking sound from somewhere.

"You done this before?" Carl called.

"Yes, but only with books."

"Thought so. You don't look like the criminal type." He waved to a younger man in blue overalls. "Bennie, get over here." He put an arm around his employee's shoulder.

"Remember that batch of paper I showed you once from the Ottoman wedding? In the corner of the supply closet."

"Yeah, I guess."

"Can you get it for me? And we're not having this conversation."

"We're not?"

"This is a . . . special job. Kind of a surprise."

"Oh." The younger man walked toward the press, rounded a corner, and disappeared.

Carl held up the plates. "We'll do a test run. Not with the high-rag paper, but something close."

He went off toward a row of 50-gallon drums and examined their labels.

Soon the pressman was back with a roll of off-white stock that looked like wallpaper. The two of them put their heads together. Finally, Bennie put on a pair of gloves and rolled one of the barrels toward the press.

Carl took out a calculator, pushed a few buttons, and put it back in his pocket. Stepping into a small, glassed-in room at the base of the press that looked like the control room of a crane, he pressed a few more.

A rumble echoed in the rafters. He took a pair of industrial noise-cancelling headphones from a hook, then found another and brought it to me.

"Put these on."

They were too big, so I held them against the sides of my head. I recalled all too well how loud these machines could be.

He returned to the control room, took the plates, and walked them to the pressman. I spent the next five minutes chewing my nails.

At last there was a hiss that sounded like steam but probably wasn't. The gears began to turn, the clacking turned to pounding, and the paper streaked through a track high overhead.

It was a short run. The motors powered down; another hiss, and Carl gave a wave to the pressman.

The foreman tore off a sheet of paper at the end of the line and presented it to me.

It was awful. Too much ink, not uncommon at the start of a run. But President Grant looked as if he'd been drinking more than usual, slurred and blurry.

"Yeah, I know," Carl said. "Not quite perfect. We'll adjust the ink flow and use the real paper."

I swallowed. "It's got to be a *lot* better."

He narrowed his eyes. "You *sure* you haven't been here before?"

"I suppose it's possible."

"Well, whatever." He went back to confer with Bennie.

A few minutes later Carl pulled a lever and pushed a button. Once more the press clacked and hummed.

Pages and pages of bills flew off the belt in a continuous sheet. Bennie laid them out to dry. We waited another 20 minutes and the process was repeated.

"The Bureau of Engraving and Printing has a trimmer that slices stacks of bills like a guillotine. We'll need to use a regular paper cutter."

He showed me a sheet. Grant's upper lip was a little smeared.

"Gets better as the run progresses."

He led me over to what looked like a giant version of one of those automatic kitty litter box cleaners.

"Feeds in here," he said. "Be careful."

"Shouldn't you be doing this?"

"I can see you're one of those 'If you want something done right, do it yourself' people."

He explained which buttons to push when, then walked away.

After a brief one-woman prayer meeting, I followed what I could remember of his instructions. The sheets vibrated; slowly the stack grew smaller.

"Hey!" yelled a voice behind me. The smell of cigar smoke mingled with the odor of ink.

It was Jimmy. "Carl! What's the matter with you? Trying to get us sued?"

The foreman came over. "I just thought—"

"No way to treat a lady, She's paying good money for this."

I breathed a sigh of relief.

Bennie trimmed the rest of the bills.

When he was done, I wrote Jimmy a check.

He picked up the first bill. "A souvenir. I'd like to frame it, but you never know when the feds might show up unannounced."

"You still look familiar," Carl said, suspicious.

"Nice doing business with you," added Jimmy.

I carried the plates and bills to the car and stashed them in the trunk.

It seemed to take forever to get back to River City. I smelled like ink and sweat. I kept telling my eyes to focus.

About halfway to relative safety I passed a car parked at a roadside diner.

The Cadillac, only newer and whiter.

Jeremy and the Nameless Girl were coming out.

I hit the steering wheel with my palm. It was always something, wasn't it?

Gunning the engine, I took a side road and came to a railroad crossing.

The arm was descending, the bell clanging.

With a gulp I thumped across the tracks just before the train came barreling through.

The engine roared like a hurricane behind me, followed by the *click-clack, click-clack* of freight cars.

Thanking God it was the longest train I'd ever seen, I set course for the motel and hoped the Cadillac wouldn't follow.

CHAPTER 24

OUT OF BREATH, I PULLED INTO THE MOTEL PARKING LOT AND hammered on Stephen and Stuart's door. The latter opened it. I could hear *Antiques Roadshow* playing on TV. Obviously it was Stuart's turn to choose the entertainment.

"Welcome back," he whispered, and ushered me inside. "How did it go in—"

The door closed behind me. "We have to get out of here. Now."

Stephen grabbed the remote and shut down some white-haired pottery appraiser. "What's up?"

"I'll explain in the car."

While they got their luggage together, I picked up the room phone and dialed Albert.

"I've got the bills," I said. "But we can't stick around. I nearly got run over by a train outrunning the people who are after us."

"How do they look?"

"He's kind of homely and oily-faced. She's in her twenties, and—"

"I meant the U.S. Grants."

"Oh." I reminded myself I was tired, not stupid. "They're good. They'd certainly fool me."

"Well, that's a disappointment. That I won't get to see them, I mean."

"Hey," said Stephen. "We're ready."

I waved him away. "Albert, you should be safe. Jeremy and the girl don't know what we're trying to do. Which means they won't be looking for you."

He sniffed. "If they are, they'll be sorry to meet my friend Mr. Remington."

"You named your rifle?"

"Of course."

"Thanks, Albert. Couldn't have done this without you."

"Don't thank me too soon. You ain't done it yet."

I hung up. After grabbing a coat I'd left in my room, I led the way to the front desk. We turned in our key cards.

"Have a nice day," said the clerk.

"Too late for that," I said.

We piled into the car and took off.

"Where to?" I asked.

"Haven't we had this conversation before?" Stephen asked.

Stuart made quote marks in the air with his fingers. "'The least likely place they'd expect us to go.' Pardon my insolence, but that's always your plan."

I adjusted the rearview mirror to look him in the eye. "The *plan* is to get enough real bills to cover the fakes. We'll have to hit every ATM from here to New Orleans and drain most of your bank account."

"No need to dwell on that."

"Good. Then it's on to Boudreaux country."

* * *

We slept, or rather spent, the night in the car at a boarded-up rest stop along the Interstate. Theoretically we took turns watching for Cadillacs, but I was the only one who stayed awake.

About 3 a.m. Stephen tapped me on the shoulder. "I have to pee," he whispered.

I grunted. "What are you, five? Just go behind the building."

"Cover me," he said, and climbed out of the back seat.

I shook my head. What was that supposed to mean?

Stuart quit snoring and sat up. "Are we there yet?"

"I swear this is like having two little kids with none of the cuteness. No, we're not there. We're here."

"Oh," he said, and settled back. By the time Stephen returned, he was sawing logs again.

At sunrise I parked at a truck stop, then looked for a pay phone. I wasn't sure they made them anymore. But I found one right outside the entrance. It wasn't a booth, just a shelf with a copy of the Yellow pages chained to the wall.

I dialed Gallagher. He was ticked.

"You know what time it is?"

"Yes," I said. "I've got the bills. We're on the road. Barely ahead of you-know-who."

He cleared his throat. "It's five in the morning."

"Can't help that. I'm at one of two remaining payphones in the continental United States, and I'm running out of change."

"What do you want from me?"

"How about we meet in Oklahoma City?"

Long pause.

"Where?"

"Let's figure that out later."

"Yes, let's. We've got all the time in the world." His sneer was practically audible.

"I'll call when we get there."

"You do that." He hung up.

I got a cup of coffee and drove on. The boys were still asleep.

About 90 minutes later a passing ambulance siren woke them up. I spotted an exit with a knot of businesses at the top.

Stephen rubbed his eyes. "I've gotta—"

"There's a 7-Eleven," I said. "Hang on."

I parked in front of the Red Box DVD machine. Stuart slowly resumed consciousness.

"You guys use the potty and get whatever you can pay for," I said. "I'll gas up."

I was squeegeeing the windshield when they emerged with a sack.

"Breakfast burritos and coffee for three," Stephen said.

I put the fuel nozzle back in its holder and tossed the receipt. "Great. Just one more thing."

"What?" Stuart asked.

"Time to use the ATM. You're collecting cash, remember? Let's start with three hundred."

He whimpered. "That's a tenth of my limit."

"Right you are. Who says artists can't do math?"

He got out his wallet and trudged toward the money dispenser.

Stephen held the bag to his nose, drew a deep breath, and smiled. "I think we should disguise the car. Go to a body shop and give it the cheapest paint job we can find."

I shook my head. "It's rented in my name. I'm in enough trouble already."

Stuart was back, looking undead. "Hope you're happy," he mumbled. "I'm drained—in more ways than one."

* * *

That night we splurged and stayed at the worst motel we could find in Ponca City, halfway between Kansas City and Oklahoma City.

"Hey," Stephen said. "It's *A Tale of Three Cities.*"

I groaned.

"Literary reference. I'm an editor, remember?"

"You're giving us a bad name."

Another night and nine ATMs later, we passed the green WELCOME TO OKLAHOMA CITY sign.

When we found a more decent motel I dialed Gallagher.

"We're here," I said.

He coughed. "I'm about fifty miles away. Let's meet near the memorial to the victims of the Oklahoma City bombing. There's a place called Heartland Chapel across the street."

Stephen's GPS app showed us the way, though it couldn't stop the traffic jam en route. When we got there we sat inside the memorial's low wooden walls, watching warily for anybody who might recognize us.

Finally Gallagher showed up, followed by a stone-faced, black-haired young man I recognized from Max's funeral.

The two of them sat down.

"This is our new friend, David," Gallagher whispered. "Max's nephew."

Stuart backed up, fear in his eyes.

I wanted to say I couldn't believe it, but couldn't risk reminding David how dangerous it was.

The young man stood up. "Too many people here."

Stephen consulted his phone. "North Harvey Avenue. There's a big stand of trees."

"Let's go," Gallagher said.

We wended our way through the foliage, then came to a clearing.

"Still too many," David said. He looked ready to run.

"No problem," Gallagher assured him. "St. Joseph's Old Cathedral is across the street."

As we stepped off the curb I noticed a marble statue of Jesus, grief-stricken, turning away from the Federal Building.

I swallowed. Too many people, too much tragedy.

Gallagher pointed to a series of black stone walls surrounding the statue. "Behind that one," he whispered.

We stood there, huddling together.

On the wall name after name of the victims were engraved.

David crossed himself.

Stuart ran his finger down the list. "At least we're not here."

"Not yet," I said.

CHAPTER 25

We sat on two benches under a tree. Mercifully, Stephen didn't bother looking up the species.

The memorial wasn't busy at the moment. Nine or ten tourists took turns posing in front of the wall of victims. A few of them actually smiled. I guess nothing's sacred anymore.

Gallagher crossed his leg over his knee and looked at David. "Tell them what you told me."

The young man leaned back and sighed. "Angel's crossed the line. She's hiding the fact that Max has had a stroke. She's running things herself."

Gallagher bent forward and tapped my shoulder. "What did I tell you?"

David kept an eye on the street adjoining the park. "She's told me in no uncertain terms that I'll never be more than a gopher as long as she's alive."

"Kind of a dead-end job, eh?" Stephen asked. "I can relate."

A razor-sharp comeback was on the tip of my tongue, but I decided it wasn't worth uttering.

"I want to bring her down," David said.

"Wouldn't it be easier to just get a better job?" Stephen asked.

David snorted. "You don't know how this works. It's a family business. If anybody knew I was doing this, I'd be dead within the hour."

"How do you plan to get the set of books?" I asked.

He lowered his voice. "They're in a safe at the mansion. I've been spending a lot of time with a girl who knows the combination."

"Isn't that a little risky?"

He nodded. "Yeah. But what you're planning with the counterfeit money could be worse."

He turned to Stuart. "Ever had acid thrown in your face?"

Stuart turned pale.

"That's almost as bad as what they'd actually do. I can't describe it. There's a lady present."

Stuart closed his eyes.

"I suggest you stay as far as you can from the mansion," David said. "I can help Carolyn get in—but not necessarily out."

Gallagher patted him on the knee. "I'll take care of that."

* * *

I checked my watch. "When do you think I should make my move?"

"Angel likes to read after dinner," David said. "Mostly financial stuff like Robert Kiyosaki and Willow Hayly."

"She's one of our biggest authors. Wouldn't be happy to know she's advising a murdering crook."

David scratched his chin. "I could introduce you as Hayly's publisher or something just to get you in. Bring a couple of books, maybe autographed. The rest will be up to you."

"I was afraid of that."

"I'll check Angel's schedule and give you a call."

He stood up. Gallagher did likewise.

"I'll be in touch, David," he said. The two of them left in opposite directions.

Stephen stuck his hands in his pockets. "Boy, I'd love to know what's worse than having acid thrown in your face."

Stuart's eyes were still closed. "Nothing personal, but put a cork in it."

We drove back to the motel, still watching for suspicious cars and faces. When we got there I called Pendleton House and asked my admin to overnight an autographed copy of Willow's memoir, *Worth It*.

"There should be one in my office," I said gently.

"I'll try. But I don't do my best under pressure."

"I know." She was perhaps the world's worst assistant, but nepotism gave her permanent job security.

I dialed Marvin. Got Tracy.

"Can't go into details," I said, "but could you pray for me?"

"'Course I can, girl. Sorry Marvin suggested the whole counterfeiting thing. Isn't there still time to back out?"

"Afraid not. Stumbling into this was my own fault."

"If you say so. But I hope your guardian angel's the kind with one of those flaming swords."

* * *

Next morning I got a call. I could barely hear the whisper. "Tomorrow night looks good."

"Is this David?"

"Let's not use names, okay?" He hung up.

Around 9:00 a.m., there was a knock at my door. It was a FedEx man with a big envelope. My overnighted book had arrived.

I called Stephen and Stuart and told them to grab their luggage. "We'll take turns driving to New Orleans."

It took just over ten hours and several pit stops to get there. Stephen and Stuart checked into a Relax Inn. Nice sentiment, but even the Hotel St. Pierre couldn't have unwound our nerves at that point.

I met David and Gallagher in a parking garage, feeling like Deep Throat if he'd just wrestled Haldeman and Ehrlichman for ten hours.

"Sure you want to go through with it?" Gallagher asked.

I nodded.

"We'll meet you there."

Taking the book and briefcase, I parked about half a mile from the estate.

David flashed the headlights on his car. I got in.

Gallagher ducked down in the back under a blanket. "Thank God I don't live in this town. It's like a steam bath without getting to take your clothes off." He coughed.

The guard, who looked like a football player turned jungle mercenary, let us through the gate.

David parked along the cobbled circular driveway. I followed him to the front door, a massive wooden monolith on brass hinges.

David used his key to open it.

We stepped inside. It looked like something out of a movie I'd seen once. *Ten Little Indians*, maybe. Winding staircase, fountain rising from a mosaic base, a portrait of Max over an empty bar.

I set the briefcase on the marble floor.

Another painting of Angel hung on the opposite wall over a bank of prehistoric-looking ferns.

"The library's upstairs," David whispered. "Are you ready?"

"Of course not."

I scanned the place for a heavenly guardian with a flaming sword.

"Not even Bart Simpson with a slingshot," I mumbled.

"Huh?"

"Nothing."

Taking a deep breath, I picked up the briefcase.

CHAPTER 26

H<small>E</small> <small>LED ME UP THE STAIRS, THE PLUSH RED CARPET SILENCING</small> my high heels. I was already dizzy, and nothing had happened yet.

After knocking gently at what looked like a solid walnut door, he adjusted his tie.

"Who is it?" called a testy female voice.

"It's me. David."

He pushed the door open. Angel was at her desk, reading. She could have been any fortyish businesswoman with an unlimited wardrobe budget.

"This is Carolyn Neville," David said. "From Pendleton Publishing in New York."

She peered over the top of her reading glasses and frowned. "I'm not interested in telling my life story, if that's what you're here for."

"So you like Willow Hayly." I placed *Worth It* next to the telephone. "This is for you."

She put down her own book and picked mine up, then flipped it open. Her face lit up—or, more precisely, seemed slightly less like a death mask.

"Hey, it's autographed. This is better than Tony Robbins."

David backed away. "Well, I'll leave you two alone." For a second, he caught my eye and gave me a look I couldn't define. Halfway between warning and panic, maybe.

The door clicked shut as I sat across from Angel.

"So you're an editor," she said. "That as boring as it sounds?"

"Umm . . . not today."

She smirked. Obviously she could hear my heart pounding, and knew exactly why.

Setting the Willow book next to the phone, she pushed her chair back from the desk. "I'm more of a numbers person myself. One who likes to get to the point."

My heart was hammering in my ears now. "I'm here on behalf of a friend. Stuart Lytle."

She squinted as if accessing a database in her head.

"Two hundred thousand," she said.

I nodded.

She picked up a black onyx paperweight. I thought she was going to pitch it at me.

"If you're here to buy time, it's too late. This is a business. I can't afford to carry this guy's debt forever."

I put the briefcase on my lap and snapped it open. "No need to do that. It wasn't easy, but we managed to raise the money."

She set down the paperweight. "You're lying."

I lifted the case and put it on the desk. "Count it if you like."

She raised an eyebrow and touched one of the bills, then picked up the phone. "Send Ernie in here."

I envisioned a hulking enforcer in a black suit with a bulge under his jacket where a holster might be. But a few moments later a sixtyish, balding man in gray slacks with a white shirt and suspenders stepped in, rubbing his wire-framed glasses with a handkerchief.

"Yes?" he asked.

"Take a look at this. Let me know in five minutes whether it comes to 200K and if it's legit."

After putting his glasses back on, he took the briefcase and left without a word.

Turning back to me, she folded her hands on the desk. The death mask was back.

"Ernie doesn't miss a trick."

"No trick," I said. But I couldn't help swallowing, and it felt like a certain paperweight was stuck in my throat.

* * *

We stared at each other, cobra and mongoose.

I wasn't the cobra.

"Suppose you think I'm some kind of monster," Angel said.

"I've . . . heard some interesting rumors."

She shrugged. "Some people can't stand a strong woman. Times have changed, but not enough. You're looking up at a glass ceiling where you work, right?"

I started to say something about how I don't yank out the fingernails of authors who don't meet their deadlines, but thought better of it.

The door opened. Ernie was back.

He set the briefcase on the desk. "It's all here. But it's not all real."

Angel sprang to her feet, looking as if someone had set her hair on fire. When she opened her mouth, the blast of profanity nearly ignited mine.

The door opened slowly. David stuck his head in.

"Everything going all right?"

I got up and backed away.

"She's a scam artist, and not a very good one," Angel said.

David's eyes widened. "That's news to me. I swear."

Avoiding my eyes, he turned and left, taking his phone from his pocket.

I grabbed the briefcase and got ready to run.

Angel picked up the paperweight. "Tell Nick to come in here."

Ernie hurried out.

Drawing back her arm, she proceeded to fling the onyx at me. I ducked and the ball hit the wall, shattering the glass on a photo of Max.

She did the same with Willow's book, but it landed on the couch.

Reaching into the top drawer of her desk, she slid out a gun and aimed it at me.

"I've got all the self-help I need right here," she said.

* * *

I hurled the briefcase at her and ran out.

An ear-splitting *kraaaak* sounded behind me. Angel was good, but it was a miss.

Suddenly, I ran into something the size of a refrigerator but not quite as steely. I smelled cologne and gunpowder.

"Ow!" it said. "Son of a—"

I looked up into the face of a beefy thug in a black suit with a bulge under his jacket where a holster might be. *Must be Nick*, I thought. His oversized hands clamped down on my shoulders, but I wriggled out of his grasp before he could make our relationship permanent.

Off balance, I righted myself and barely kept from tripping as I descended the staircase.

As I got to the bottom the front door flew open and Gallagher rushed in, revolver held high. His eyes were wild.

David backed into a corner. I was beginning to wonder whose side he was on.

From behind me another shot was fired. Nick, I guessed.

Gallagher grunted, then swayed, then collapsed on an expensive-looking area rug.

No time to help him. Panting, I leapt over the body.

Another shot whizzed past me, blasting a Chinese urn to dust.

The night air hit me in the face like a load of wet laundry.

Spotting my car in the distance, I ran for it.

CHAPTER 27

I drove like a maniac, trying not to think about Gallagher lying on the reddening carpet.

The sudden *BLAAAAAAA* of an oncoming semi's horn caught my attention. Squinting against its headlights, I swerved right and bounced on the shoulder like a jetliner minus its landing gear.

The truck kept barreling down that open road. I could imagine its driver calling in my license plate number.

Momentarily releasing my grip on the steering, I felt the car veer to the right. I'd shot the alignment.

I wasn't looking forward to forcing the wheel leftward for the rest of the trip, but didn't have much choice. We wouldn't have time to drop in at a Firestone.

Reaching the motel, I pounded on the boys' door. Stephen answered. "Hey, you're alive. How'd it go?"

"Pack your bags."

Stuart looked over Stephen's shoulder. "*Again?*"

"Yeah, we seem to do this a lot," Stephen added. "And then we argue about where to go next."

I threw up my hands. "What part of 'Pack your bags' don't

you understand? For all I know, Nick could be right behind me."

"Who's Nick?"

"I'll tell you in the car if he doesn't kill us first."

Mumbling, Stephen closed the door. I dashed to my room and scooped my possessions into a motel laundry bag.

We checked out and piled into the car. When I started to leave the parking lot, Stephen whistled.

"You're out of alignment. What did you do, run over somebody?"

"No, but I wanted to."

Back on the Interstate, I looked in the rearview mirror at Stuart.

"Angel's got your money and the counterfeit bills." He stared straight ahead.

All at once he reached toward the door. "This is where I get off," he said, sounding almost hypnotized.

"What are you, crazy?" Stephen yelled, grabbing his shirt. When I hit the child safety lock to keep him from falling onto the pavement, the car careened to the left. A horn beeped behind me.

Shaking his head, Stephen let him go. "Dude, you're psycho."

"I know. But I'd rather end it now than wait for them to end it for me."

"Can't afford to lose my best children's author," I said.

He sank into his seat, silent.

Stephen looked out the window. "*Now* will you tell us what happened?"

I described it all, right down to the onyx paperweight. And, of course, what appeared to be Gallagher's last stand.

"Is he dead?" Stephen asked.

"Not sure. If he isn't already, he will be soon."

"So will we if we don't find a new place to hide," Stuart said.

* * *

A half hour later we paused to gas up at a truck stop. "This time *you* pump and pay," I told Stephen.

"I can't afford it," he whined.

"How much is your life worth?"

"Is that a threat?"

"Take it any way you like."

I headed toward the convenience store, hoping to find a pay phone. There was one, but when I picked up the receiver it was clear that vaudeville and chivalry weren't the only things that were dead.

I'd have to chance calling David on my cell. It connected, but there was no answer.

I wondered whether Angel had guessed he'd betrayed her.

Going inside, I perused the shelves for something to keep me awake and comfort my twisting stomach. I ended up with a canned latte and a package of donut holes.

Back in the car I waited while Stephen and Stuart foraged for sustenance. I looked toward the highway. Were Jeremy and the Nameless Girl after us? Did Nick ever leave the estate?

I took out my phone and called Marvin.

"Cranberry! Thank God you're okay. Wasn't sure I'd hear from you again."

"Me neither." I gave him the same rundown I'd given my colleagues.

There was a long silence. "Sounds like everything's fallen apart. I never should have suggested—"

"Seemed like a good idea at the time. Even to me."

The back doors opened. Stephen and Stuart climbed in. I could smell nachos.

I put Marvin on speaker. "Let's take a vote. Where do you think we should go?"

"Is Pluto an option?" Stephen asked. He started crunching.

"I guess Florida's out," Marvin said. "Not that we wouldn't love seeing you folks again."

I opened my can of fancy coffee. "So's Idaho."

"And Manhattan," Stuart said.

I unwrapped the donut holes. "What about going back to the Amish community?"

Marvin cleared his throat. "Honey, that sounds *way* too dangerous. Unless you can convince the Boudreauxs you've gone somewhere else."

Stuart shook his head and unscrewed the cap from an orange soda. "It would be even better if we could convince the family we're *dead*."

"Are you serious?" Marvin asked.

"It worked for the Boudreauxs, didn't it?"

* * *

I opened my mouth for rebuttal, but something white caught my eye.

A Cadillac was pulling up to a nearby pump. *The* Cadillac.

Jeremy got out, looking exhausted.

"We'll talk later, Marvin," I whispered and stuck the phone back in my pocket.

"Seatbelts," I said. We took off, the car still trying to convince me to turn right.

I had to assume Jeremy had spotted us and would follow, but couldn't be sure.

"It'll be hard to fake our own deaths without actually

dying," I said. "Stephen, can you find somewhere we can slow down enough to jump from the car and let it go over a cliff or something? I can't believe I actually said that, but it's the best worst idea we've got."

He ate the last of his nachos and started searching on his phone.

Stuart tapped the buckle on his seatbelt. "Should have let me jump when you had the chance. Seriously."

I checked the mirror. "White Cadillac about a mile behind us."

"Got it," Stephen said. "Take this next road to the right."

I let go of the steering wheel and let the car have its way.

"I'm trying not to think about what's going to happen when the rental company hears their car has burned to a crisp," I said.

Stephen snorted. "Probably will, given the full gas tank. But they won't find any bodies—unless we screw up."

"Maybe they'll think we were thrown clear and survived. They'll search for us. But they won't know we've gone to Pennsylvania."

Stephen looked at his phone. "Slow down." He paused. "Are they still behind us?"

"Yeah, about half a mile."

"Okay. There's a sharp left turn and a ravine about 300 feet ahead. We'll have to bail out before that."

I swallowed and sent up a quick prayer. Were I Catholic, I'd be grabbing my dashboard St. Christopher.

Slowing to about 15 miles per hour, I unsnapped my seatbelt and hoisted my purse on my shoulder.

"We'll have to make a run for it," Stephen said. "Into those trees on the right."

Glancing in the mirror, I saw Stuart clutching his suitcase, pale as parchment.

"I'll count down from ten," Stephen said. "Try to hit the ground running."

We were nearing the cliff. I gripped the handle of my overnight bag.

"*Three . . . two . . . one*," Stephen said.

We flung the doors open. "*Now!*"

I rolled through the weeds, hoping I'd stop before I ran out of ground. Stuart was on my side, and hit the dirt like a bale of hay.

I helped him up. Stephen was dusty but apparently unharmed.

The three of us fled toward the trees. Stuart was limping.

The car sailed over the edge, hit the rocks, and burst into flame.

CHAPTER 28

WE HUDDLED IN THE TREES. I HUGGED MYSELF, NUMB. Stephen and Stuart looked at each other.

"Cool explosion," Stephen said.

Stuart just stared.

The swish of brush and pop of gravel made us shrink behind what looked like a pine. Slowly the Cadillac approached.

Jeremy and the Nameless Girl got out and peered over the edge.

He swore, no doubt feeling cheated of the chance to kill us himself. She craned her neck but apparently saw nothing.

He took out his phone.

"We're at the edge of a cliff outside town. They've gone over. Car blew up. Can't be any survivors."

For a moment he listened, then stuck the phone back in his pocket.

"You look disappointed," the girl said.

He swore. "Don't worry about me. Just do your freakin' job, okay?"

"Will you please *chill?* It's like riding around with that guy in *Pulp Fiction.*"

"John Travolta?"

She nodded.

"I'll take that as a compliment."

They climbed in the car and took off.

Stuart sagged against the tree, eyes shut.

"Can you walk?" I asked.

"Not very far."

Stephen scanned the ground. "Anybody seen my phone?"

"Maybe it fell out when you hit the ground."

He wandered over to a clump of foliage and felt around with his shoe. "Wish I had a flashlight."

I took out my own phone and called him. Jackson Browne's "Running on Empty" burst out of the bushes.

"Ah," he said, and started punching buttons. "Wonder if we can get an Uber out here."

He frowned. "Only one bar."

After three tries, he gave up. "Probably wouldn't come out here anyway."

"Up for a hike?" I asked, trying in vain to clean myself off with spit and a Kleenex.

Stuart groaned.

"Stay here if you like," I said. "If we make it back to civilization, we'll send someone back to get you."

He grunted. "I don't think the outdoors is as great as it's cracked up to be."

"Me neither."

The three of us started walking back toward the highway, dragging what was left of our luggage behind us.

* * *

The lights of the truck stop glowed in the distance like a desert oasis, or at least the Desert Inn Casino in Las Vegas. I'd never been there, but I'd seen pictures. Lots of red neon.

I felt every inch of the mile-and-a-half trip back. Stuart's limp was worse but he looked too tired to complain.

The closer we got, the more I smelled exhaust fumes and chicken nuggets. Stephen took a deep breath and smiled.

"Sometimes truckers pick up hitchhikers," he said. "Or at least they used to on TV."

We reached the edge of the concrete pad with the pumps. Stephen bent down and picked up a dirty white piece of cardboard next to a puddle on the ground. "Hold this," he said.

I did, for a second, then leaned it against a telephone pole.

He went into the convenience center. Stuart was trying to hold his breath.

Finally, Stephen came out. "Got a black Sharpie. They've got *everything* in there."

We watched as he wrote PENNSYLVANIA OR BUST on the poster board.

"Nobody says 'or bust' anymore," I muttered.

For the next 45 minutes, we stood near the Interstate entrance and took turns holding up the sign.

No takers.

"Show a little more leg," Stephen told me.

"This is me ignoring you."

"I'll try Uber again."

"Or Lyft."

He smiled. "I've got bars."

Somebody must have answered. He described our location, then paused. Face falling, he hung up.

"They don't come out here. Too far from a city, even the suburbs."

"What now?" Stuart asked, holding his nose.

"Beats me."

"There's a motel next to the truck stop," Stephen said.

I shuddered. "Looks like a haven for hookers and a breeding ground for bacteria."

Just then a huge Mack semi rumbled to a halt in front of us, brakes hissing. A tough-looking woman with a red face, braids like hemp rope, and a bandana around her neck stuck her head out the window.

* * *

"Take you far as Oklahoma City," she croaked.

I tossed the poster away. "Thank you."

We clambered into the cab. It was cramped, but we managed to find just enough room to stow our luggage. I could hear a dog whining in the back.

"That's Queenie," the driver said. "Pay no attention to her. She's a big baby. Just got fed."

She stuck out her hand. "I'm Paula."

We introduced ourselves.

She put the mammoth vehicle in gear and checked the rearview mirror. "I'm an independent trucker. Otherwise I'd have to fill out a bunch of paperwork to let you ride with me." She shook her head. "God bless the Department of Transportation."

With a rumble the truck began moving like a barge leaving the dock.

"You don't look like typical hitchhikers," she said.

I nudged Stephen's elbow out of my ribs. "Our car suddenly gave up the ghost. Had to leave it behind."

We rode in silence for a while. I watched the lights flash past the window.

"Mind if I turn on the radio?" Paula asked, her fingers hovering over the button.

"Go right ahead," I said.

It was an all-news station. After a slew of commercials for Rosland Capital and Gold Bond Medicated Powder, there was a story about a car on fire. I leaned forward.

" . . . in Hard Rock Canyon," the reporter said. "Emergency vehicles on the scene. Probably no survivors."

Paula sighed and changed channels.

The rest of us looked at each other. Except for Queenie, who whined in the back.

"Shut up, you mutt," the driver said. "Can't take you anywhere."

I closed my eyes. Another show was coming on. Paula turned up the sound.

Ah, a talk-show conspiracy theorist. I tried not to listen as he proceeded to hold forth on the coming war with the armies of Atlantis.

CHAPTER 29

WE REACHED OKLAHOMA CITY AT 6:00 A.M., BLEARY-EYED. Except for Paula, who appeared ready to do battle with Neptune's minions.

Her eyes were a little too shiny as she picked another truck stop. Rolling up to a propane tank, she braked with a hiss.

She glanced back at the dog, who was asleep. "Good luck."

"It's been real," I said.

Stephen mumbled something I couldn't make out. Stuart gathered his belongings and nearly fell onto the pavement.

Taking a look at our luggage, the waitress gave us menus and bustled to a corner booth. I could smell ketchup and bacon grease. The place was crowded, and not just with drivers. A busload of high school drum-and-bugle team members, half out of uniform, packed three tables. Two middle-aged chaperones developing PTSD tried unsuccessfully to keep them from making spit wads of straw wrappers and blow-gunning them at each other.

We sat down. "Hash browns look good," Stephen said loudly.

Stuart studied the menu. "Grits with redeye gravy. Seems geographically misplaced."

Stephen put his menu down. "Isn't that your phone?"

"*What?*" I called over the din.

"Your ringtone."

I looked down at my purse. "Oh."

I checked caller ID.

"Uh-oh."

"Problem?" Stuart asked.

"Car rental company. Not looking forward to *that* conversation. Also can't let anybody know we're alive." I let it ring. Eventually it gave up.

The waitress returned and took our orders. English muffin and jam for me, hash browns and eggs for Stephen. Stuart couldn't make up his mind yet.

"We've got twenty hours to go until Pennsylvania," Stephen announced.

I sighed. "Should we try hitchhiking again?"

"Seems to be our only choice."

"Eggs Benedict," Stuart said, and closed his menu.

Eventually we all got our food, splitting the bill. Stationing ourselves near the propane tank, this time without a sign, we stuck out our thumbs and looked hopeful.

"No cardboard?" Stuart said.

"Couldn't find any," said Stephen.

After an hour without a bite, I shook my head. "Time to put on our Amish outfits," I said.

"Oh, that'll do it," Stephen said. "People will think it's a fraternity hazing."

"We're too old for that," I said. "They might think we've just lost a bet."

We went back to the bathroom and changed. For the next half hour we got mostly stares from passersby. But finally a big Peterbilt rig pulled up just past the pumps and idled.

There was a fish symbol near the USDOT number on the cab door. "Oh, look," Stephen said. "One of *your* people, Carolyn."

"Maybe he just likes catching trout."

"No, he's a Christian. Fishermen have bumper stickers that say things like 'The Rodfather.'"

A guy who resembled Neil Young in his heyday stuck his head out the window. He wore a blue stocking cap.

"Looks like you need a ride." I could swear he stifled a snicker.

We squeezed into the seat. "Glad there's no dog," Stephen whispered.

"My name's Greg." He shifted gears and slowly circled toward the highway.

"You Amish?" he asked.

"Well, not exactly," I said.

He scratched the side of his nose. "So why are you dressed like that?"

Stephen leaned forward. "We're . . . doing research for a book. It's called . . . *The Year of Living Amishly.*"

I gave him a look but didn't say anything.

"When I'm on the road I visit the Trucker's Chapel. Helps me stay on the straight and narrow."

"Bless you, my son," Stephen said. I kicked him.

"DOT rules don't let me drive twenty hours straight," Greg said. "So I'll be stopping along I-70E. Probably sleep in the cab, but for you I'll park at a cheap motel I know of."

Stephen took out his phone. "What's it called?"

"Silver Moon."

Stephen looked it up. "Not even listed. *That's* a good sign."

"Are Amish folks regular hitchhikers?"

"Not in my experience," I admitted.

Stuart grunted. "It was this or driving a buggy—and we haven't got the time for that."

"What're you going to do when you get there?"

"Visit friends and try not to get them killed," I said.

He nodded. "Two admirable goals." He tapped the wheel with both index fingers. "Can I pray for you?"

"Do you *have* to?" Stephen asked.

"He's doing us a favor," I growled.

"Just don't close your eyes," Stephen muttered.

The driver chuckled, then filed a brief request for protection.

I kept my eyes open too, checking the side mirror.

* * *

We got to the Silver Moon around suppertime.

It was surrounded by flatlands, but Swiss-looking yellow dingbats decorated its peeling blue balconies.

Gently Greg brought the Peterbilt to a halt on the edge of a vacant lot nearby.

He stayed in the cab; we checked in. The clerk was a girl who looked about 14, with a black sweatshirt and gray circles under her eyes.

"We'd like two rooms," I said. My gaze dropped to the counter, where sat a greasy paper plate, circled by flies. After fishing around in my purse for hand sanitizer, I applied it liberally.

We flipped a coin to see who got which room. I lost.

It smelled like it had been attacked by a giant Glad Hawaiian Breeze plug-in. I decided not to turn back the blanket until it was too dark to see. No use trying to find a better place. The nearest Stephen could locate was 75 miles away.

I tugged the curtain pull cord; it refused to budge.

Just as well. Last thing I needed was to be spotted by anybody who thought I was dead.

I lifted the receiver of the room phone. At least I got a dial tone.

Tried to call David again. No answer.

This time I left a message.

The three of us went to dinner at the only place around. Louie's, where there was no wait, a whole swarm of flies, and no other customers.

The waitress, who was using a walker, looked us up and down.

"I'm starting to feel weird in this outfit," Stuart whispered. "Going to change in the morning."

We sat down. "Wonder whether David has gotten into the safe," Stephen said.

"Not sure he's still *alive*," I replied.

Stuart picked up the HEY, KIDS! COLOR ME! paper placemat on the table and turned it to the blank side. Choosing a black crayon from the little box, he proceeded to draw caricatures of Stephen and me.

He held them up. "Not my best work. Consider the medium and circumstances."

"I like the one of me," Stephen said.

Mine made me look like Melissa McCarthy, which was off by about 50 pounds. I just smiled.

Stuart finished by drawing Angel from memory. He gave her horns.

We all ordered the most inexpensive item on the menu, meatloaf.

When it came time to pay the bill, the waitress slowly took it to the back room and returned several minutes later.

"Credit card's been rejected," she said, handing it over.

"Maybe they heard you're dead," Stephen whispered, and pulled out his Visa. "As Mark Twain said, 'The reports of my death have been greatly exaggerated.'"

I sighed. "Not mine. In my case, they're merely premature."

* * *

After dinner, back in my room, I finally got a call from David.

"Gallagher's dead," he said.

CHAPTER 30

I ALMOST DROPPED THE PHONE.

It didn't surprise me, having seen Gallagher shot down. But suddenly I felt alone, unprotected.

I put the receiver back to my ear. "What did they do with the body? Surely they didn't call the police."

He was silent for a moment. "Don't think you want to know. Let's just say the family and their favorite mortuary took care of things."

"Man had no relatives I know of. Guess the Boudreauxs can get away with anything they want."

"Almost got the set of books from the safe last night, but Ernie walked in on me."

"We're in Oklahoma, on our way to Pennsylvania. We'll be laying low in an Amish community."

"Amish. The ones with the buggies?"

"Right."

"You're putting me on."

"Hey, we've done it before."

"God, I can't imagine pretending to be Amish, let alone actually *being* that way. For one thing, I'm allergic to hay."

"Like on *Green Acres*? The TV show?"

"Never heard of it."

"How about *Witness*? The movie."

"Haven't seen it. Must be about shutting an informer up. You trying to make me feel worse, or what?"

"Sorry." He seemed pretty thin-skinned for a gangster. Maybe it was a family trait.

"I'll try the safe again tomorrow," he said. "Angel or Ernie or somebody's going to wise up. Can't keep doing this forever."

The line went dead.

I hung up. "Neither can I."

* * *

Next morning I told Stephen and Stuart about Gallagher and David. Stuart shook his head sadly. I started to choke up, remembering the former agent's gruff way of keeping an eye on us. I even missed his cough.

Stuart went to the window and parted the blinds with his fingers. "Everything depends on David now. The longer we have to spend in Amish country, the greater the chance we'll be ambushed and take our hosts with us."

"We've got to leave. But no more hitchhiking."

Stephen took out his phone. "Plane, train, or automobile?"

"I'm thinking bus."

"As in Greyhound?" Stuart asked.

"Let's try Trailways. Heard they're cheaper."

Two hours later we hit the road. We used Stephen's card, but only after I promised to reimburse him.

The bus was half empty. Most of the passengers were asleep. The place smelled of sweat and gasoline.

"Spread out," I told the boys. "I'm sick of being stuffed in the cab of a truck."

"Fine," Stephen said. "Be that way."

I sat about two-thirds of the way back, by a window. Stowing my purse under the seat, I leaned back, closed my eyes, and felt the vertebrae in my neck pop.

"Can I sit here?" a high-pitched voice asked.

I opened my eyes and turned right. A boy about eleven, apparently traveling alone, stood in the aisle with his hands in his pockets. Skinny, hair the color of a new penny, wearing a black Sonic the Hedgehog sweatshirt. He wore a green backpack.

"Name's Michael. You remind me of my third grade teacher, Mrs. Lovelace."

"Great."

"I'm on my way to Philadelphia to spend a month with my aunt and see the Liberty Bell."

"Wonderful."

"So, can I sit here?"

I looked around. The place was starting to fill up.

I sighed. "Yeah. Just try to keep yourself entertained."

"Okay."

The driver took his seat and shut the door. With a rumble the bus rolled away from the station.

The kid kept his promise for a mile or so. After that he wouldn't shut up, which explained why his mother was sending him several states away.

"Let's play the license plate game," he said.

I groaned. "You start." I shut my eyes again.

"Tennessee," he said.

I grunted.

"Iowa."

This went on for five minutes. I couldn't stand any more.

"You win," I said.

"Awesome! So why are you dressed up like a pioneer or whatever?"

"I feel safer that way."

He looked around and saw Stephen and Stuart. "Didn't those guys get on the bus with you?"

"Uh-uh."

"Are they afraid of something too?"

"Could be."

"I'm not scared of anything," he whispered.

I stared out the window. A white Cadillac was passing us. Couldn't tell whether it was anybody we knew.

Just in case, I ducked down. "Can you trade me places?"

"How come?"

"I'd feel even safer."

He shrugged and we traded.

I sneaked to the back and warned Stephen and Stuart to stay out of sight.

"Oh, crap," Stephen said. They sank into their seats.

Returning to my place, I dialed David. I had no choice, there being a lack of pay phones in the vicinity.

He answered.

"Is it likely that Jeremy and the girl are on our trail?" I whispered.

"All I know is they're not in New Orleans."

"Talk to you later. I hope."

I turned to Michael. "Did you see the license on that Cadillac?"

"Sure. Louisiana. I know it from the pelican and flowers. Says, 'Sportsman's Paradise'."

I swallowed. "Back in a minute."

Making my way to Stephen and Stuart, I proceeded to kneel in the aisle next to them.

"I suggest we hide in the restrooms for a while."

"Why?" Stuart asked.

"Just do it, okay?"

We did, but soon other passengers were pounding on the doors.

We went back to our seats.

"Wow," Michael said. "You must have *really* needed to go to the bathroom."

I nodded. "But not for the reason you think."

He winked. "Smoking, right?"

"You won't tell anybody, will you?"

"Not if you give me five dollars."

I found the hush money in my purse and handed it over, wondering why I still wished I had children.

* * *

After what seemed like a geologic age, we pulled into the Philadelphia Bus Station. I waved to Michael as he headed for the taxi stand. "Don't worry," he called. "I'll be fine. And thanks for all the money."

Looking over our shoulders to see whether we were being followed, we found a rental agency and got the cheapest compact we could find on Stephen's card.

Taking back roads, we drove to the Stoltzfus place.

The three of us were bathed in yellow porch light as I knocked on the door.

Aaron answered.

He stepped back, astonished. "I thought I'd never see you again."

I almost smiled. "Not sure what you mean by that."

The door opened wider. The Bishop peered around it and straightened his glasses.

"The prodigals return," he said, looking as if the gift of hospitality had finally slipped from his grasp. "Lord help us."

CHAPTER 31

THEY INVITED US INSIDE, OF COURSE. THEY HAD TO.

We sat on the couch while the Bishop's wife got us lemonade. "They're still after us," I said. "You know what happens when you disturb a hornet's nest?"

"Only too well," the old man said.

"They shot the man from the FBI who was helping us. He found a member of the family to look for their financial records. That could put them in jail. You and God willing, we need to stay here again. But just until we have the books."

The Bishop bowed his head, no doubt seeking divine guidance. After a few moments he nodded. "Seventy times seven," he said.

Stephen accepted a glass of lemonade. "Don't have to stay *that* long—490 days."

I got the next drink and nodded at Mrs. Stoltzfus. "That's the number of times a follower of Jesus should forgive someone who sins against him. Or her."

"Not that this is a sin," the old man said. "Not exactly."

"More of a gross imposition," his wife muttered, and handed Stuart his glass.

After a few more minutes of awkward conversation, we rose to take our things back to the barn.

"You are welcome to join us for supper. You don't mind leftovers?"

"Not *yours*," Stephen said.

After a dinner of ham, brown bread, and string beans, Aaron stood behind my chair. "Care to take a walk?" he whispered.

My heart beat a little faster. *Don't get your hopes up*, I told myself.

We walked to the spot where we'd last met to watch the stars and distant village lights. The only sound was cattle mooing. I wondered how long those lights and sounds had remained the same in this land that time forgot.

Finally Aaron spoke. "I've been spending time with a young lady named Susanna."

I blinked. A wave of jealousy and sadness washed over me. Unpleasant surprise.

"I'm so happy for you," I said. I had to. "What's she like?"

He folded his arms across his chest. "You know Proverbs 31?"

"Not by heart."

"Well, Susanna fits the description of the Proverbs 31 woman."

"Virtuous."

He nodded. "Her price is far above rubies."

"I suppose she looks for wool and stuff and sews her own clothes."

"Sure does. Gives meat to her household. Knows how to invest, or would if we had any money."

"Lays her hand to the spindle?"

"Of course."

"Does she work out?"

He raised an eyebrow. "Excuse me?"

"As I recall, she's supposed to gird her loins with strength and pump up her arms."

"Amish women get plenty of exercise. They don't need to join muscle clubs."

"I think you mean health clubs."

I gazed up at the stars. "That's a glowing review. But how about the Song of Solomon? Anything there apply to her?"

Even in the moonlight, I could see him blush.

He walked me back to the barn. "Sleep well," he said, and touched the brim of his hat.

Stephen and Stuart, lying on the straw, sat up when I came in.

"Carolyn's got a boyfriend," Stephen said in a singsong voice.

"Not anymore."

"Then you admit you *had* one."

"Yeah, but that was a long time ago."

He lay back down.

Glancing up, I got an idea. A bale of hay was dangling from a hook over his head.

I unwound the rope from a nearby post and let it go.

The hay plummeted and hit him in the stomach.

"Holy crap!" Doubling up, he started sneezing.

Stuart stifled a laugh.

"'Night, boys. See you in the morning."

I went to my corner, lay down, and wished I could do it again.

* * *

We were awakened at dawn by a crowing rooster, followed immediately by the sound of my phone. The Stoltzfus household had a landline, but I decided to use my own. If Jeremy and the girl were close enough to monitor my calls, it was already too late.

"It's David. I've finally got the financial records from the safe."

"Thank God."

"Have to get them to the FBI, but can't be seen there myself. Going to photocopy key pages and hire a courier to take them to Chicago. That'll take several hours."

"Okay."

"In the meantime, I heard Angel on the phone yesterday, going ballistic over something she heard. 'I'll take care of it myself,' she said."

"Uh-oh."

"Maybe it's got nothing to do with you. Whatever it was, she packed up and left an hour later."

He hung up.

With a grunt Stephen rose painfully from his bed in the straw.

Sneezing, he pointed at me. "Hope you're happy!"

He found a rag next to a milk pail and blew his nose.

"Ecstatic," I said, and headed for the coop. It was my turn to feed the chickens.

* * *

We breakfasted on scrapple, a dish made of pig parts, corn meal, and flour. The Bishop's wife called it "pan rabbit."

It tasted better than it sounds but not much. "Reminds me of Scooby," I said, but nobody knew what I was talking about.

"Got a call this morning," I said, and told them David's news.

The Bishop led a prayer for David's safety and our own.

The rest of the morning was spent on chores. We were

out there with Aaron, dragging the irrigation system in the field, when two cars pulled up.

One was the white Cadillac.

From the other, a black Lincoln Town Car with tinted windows, a man with a gun drawn emerged.

It was Nick from the Boudreaux mansion. After surveying the scene, he motioned to his passenger.

Out stepped Angel, squinting in the sun.

We froze.

She walked toward me, picking her way carefully among the dirt clods, turning up her nose at the smell of manure.

She glared at me, not saying anything.

CHAPTER 32

"DON'T LIKE HAVING TO CLEAN UP OTHER PEOPLE'S MESSES," Angel said. "The flight from New Orleans was overbooked, and the drive from the airport was a bore."

She stepped toward Aaron, then circled him like a hawk. Obviously she liked what she saw.

"What's your name, honey?" she asked.

"Aaron."

"I could use a young man like you. In more ways than one."

Blushing, he lowered his head.

She laughed. "I can see it wouldn't work out, plowboy. So back off. Don't get any ideas about rescuing these thieves. 'Thou shalt not steal,' right?"

He nodded.

Nick ambled toward Stuart, followed by Jeremy and the Nameless Girl.

"Don't suppose you have my money, Mr. Lytle," Angel said.

"No."

"Then you leave me no choice."

Aaron leaned toward me. "One always has a choice," he whispered.

Angel frowned. "You care to share that with the rest of the class?"

"No, Ma'am."

"Guess we can take care of this right here. Can't have my customers thinking they can get away with grand larceny."

She turned to her colleagues.

"Take out the trash, please," she said, and climbed back in the car.

* * *

"Hands on your heads," Nick ordered. "Kneel on the ground."

We did so, our knees sinking in the mud. I was going into tachycardia, my usual response to death threats and techno pop.

"Let Aaron go," I said. "He's got nothing to do with this."

"He does now."

"The FBI's on its way."

He snorted. "Sure it is."

"They've got your financial records. Proof of tax evasion."

He lowered his gun, jogged to the car, and said something through the window to his boss.

She flung the door open. He jumped back, nearly falling.

"What's this about records?" she yelled at me.

"It's over, Angel."

Stephen grinned. "Like Al Capone."

"They can't get you for murder," I said, "but the IRS will be very interested in the contents of your safe."

She got out her phone and stabbed at the screen.

"Who's this? Where's David?" There was a pause. "What do you mean, you don't know?"

Swearing, she hung up and paced back and forth.

Angel waggled her fingers dismissively in our direction. "Okay, take them with us. We'll need some bargaining chips."

Nick grabbed my shoulder and yanked me to my feet. "You heard the lady."

She got back in the car, this time in the driver's seat.

CHAPTER 33

THREE DARK BLUE UNMARKED CARS THUMPED AND BUMPED their way down the rutted dirt road toward us.

Stephen struggled to his feet and leaned against a tree. "What took you so long?" he yelled.

Stuart gasped. "Reinforcements?"

"Oh, yeah."

"Theirs or ours?"

"Ours, I hope."

Seven heavily-armed men and one woman wearing bulletproof vests clambered out. The tallest one swung his automatic rifle back and forth like a reaper's scythe. He was built like Dwayne Johnson, but his glasses made him look like Napoleon Dynamite.

"Federal agents!" he shouted. "Throw your weapons on the ground!"

Nick, Jeremy, and the Nameless Girl glanced at each other, hesitating.

Napoleon Johnson stamped his foot. "Now!"

One at a time, they dropped their guns.

It hurt to get up. One of my shoes was half buried in

muck. Aaron straightened, looking angrier than any Amishman had a right to.

Stephen helped Stuart up.

The Lincoln's engine roared to life.

"Crap," Stephen said. "She's getting away."

Two agents whirled and pointed their guns at the car. The backs of their jackets yelled *FBI* in yellow.

I gripped my leg and yanked. My shoe popped out of the gunk with a sucking sound.

For reasons I didn't quite understand, I grabbed my purse and ran toward the car. Maybe I couldn't stand the thought of losing after all we'd been through. Or perhaps I wasn't thinking at all.

"Ma'am, don't!" the nearest FBI man said.

"Sorry," I said, panting. "Got the greatest respect for law enforcement. Next time you guys call raising money, count on me for a donation."

Grabbing the front passenger door and jerking, I climbed in just as the car got seriously underway.

Squeezing the wheel with both hands, Angel swore. Not in a general way. It was very personal.

The wheel shook as she guided the Lincoln in reverse to the highway. I belted myself in.

Pausing just long enough to fumble a pair of sunglasses from the glove compartment, she stomped on the accelerator and spun with a screech onto the asphalt.

* * *

"What the [expletive deleted] do you think you're doing?" Angel asked.

"Darned if I know."

"Those agents may have bulletproof vests. You sure don't."

We whizzed past a horse and buggy with a triangular red

sign on the back. Keeping her eyes on the road, she manhandled a gun from her own purse.

"It was David, wasn't it?" she asked. "How much did you pay him? I thought you were broke."

I started to answer. But I couldn't put David in more danger by revealing his complicity.

"If you think you're putting me in prison, forget it. I've got more lawyers than Capone ever did, and better. And if you think I'm going to let you out of this car alive, you're a bigger idiot than I thought."

She pulled into the passing lane again. Hitting the gas, she barely avoided an oncoming semi, which condemned her with a blast like a foghorn.

I reached over and tried to wrestle the gun from her hand. The muscles in her forearms tensed in sharp relief, and her fingernails drew blood.

"Trying to get us both killed?" she asked.

With a *kraaaak* the gun went off, shattering the windshield.

The car swerved. With her left hand, she took hold of the wheel and forced the car hard to the right.

The Lincoln sailed gracefully into a ditch, water gushing in where the windshield used to be.

I unbuckled. So did she, but with more profane commentary.

The car sank just deep enough to submerge our chins.

The engine choked, shuddered, then died.

I opened my door; the water rushed in like high tide at the Bay of Fundy.

Dragging my purse, I made my way through the mire and grass to a barbed-wire fence up the hill.

* * *

A cow mooed ahead of me. I turned to see Angel stumble out on her side.

She held the gun and aimed at me. I ducked, as if that would do any good.

There was a click.

That was it. No firing. Apparently the thing was too wet.

She threw the gun aside and waded through the water.

I backed away, trying not to touch the barbed wire.

"It's over," she said through gritted teeth.

"Probably."

"Lady, you obviously don't know the first thing about me. I didn't get where I am by waving a white flag."

The sound of squealing brakes met my ears.

One of the FBI cars halted on the other side of the ditch. Out climbed a pair of agents, a man and a woman, with assault weapons drawn.

"Freeze, Angel," the woman said, and not softly.

The cow mooed again.

Muddy and dripping, I stepped back from the fence and collapsed in the grass.

CHAPTER 34

ANGEL DIDN'T MOVE.

The female agent handcuffed her. "Angel Boudreaux, you have the right to remain silent . . ."

"I know all that."

She looked at me, smirking. "I'll be out before the sun goes down. But you'll be running the rest of your life."

The officer tugged her arm. "Get in the car."

"You okay, Ma'am?" the male agent asked me.

"Sure, considering I just received a death threat."

Another car pulled up. I saw Stephen, Stuart, and Aaron inside, an agent at the wheel. They piled out.

Stephen took one look at me and shook his head.

Stuart was panting, hand over his heart. I started to reach for my phone to dial 911, but opted to wait until he actually fell over.

Frowning, Aaron leaped the ditch and helped me up.

"You look like a horse that got rode too hard and put away wet," he said. "Or just an Amish girl who never learned how to swim."

Feeling dizzy, I took his hand to steady myself.

He looked down and pulled away, clearly embarrassed.

"That barbed wire got you pretty good," he said.

"I'll live." I paused. "We passed one of your brethren on the road. Didn't slow us down a bit."

Suddenly my knees buckled. My head seemed to float off my neck. I started to sway.

"Lord have mercy," he said, catching me. Strong arms carried me through the ditch and back to the car.

Stuart spread his coat on the back seat. I got in.

The FBI car with Angel in it headed for the highway.

My phone rang. It was Marvin.

"Cranberry, you dead yet?"

"What?"

"You were gonna fake your own expiration, remember?"

I shook myself, trying to clear my head. "Did that. It worked, more or less. The FBI swung its sweet chariot low. They're taking Angel and her unheavenly host across the Jordan."

"Honey, I don't know what you're talking about, but sounds like you could use a week or two down here. In somebody *else's* condo."

"I'll call back later and tell you all about it, okay?"

"See that you do."

I hung up.

Aaron squeezed into the back seat. His shoulder was warm against my soggy side.

Stephen got in the front passenger seat and turned to the agent. "Can I try on your bulletproof vest? It's just so cool."

"Negative," he said, and started the car. "Get your own on the Internet."

* * *

We went back to the Stoltzfus place.

The Bishop's wife opened the door, panic in her eyes.

"It's all right," Aaron said. "The English criminals are on their way to jail."

She relaxed. *Melted* might be a better word.

We stepped over the threshold. The Bishop rose from his rocking chair. Without warning he led a prayer of thanks. I could barely get my eyes shut in time.

"You need a clean outfit," his wife told me when it was over. "I'll find you one." She disappeared into a bedroom.

"Guess I can go," the FBI agent said. "You folks will have to—"

His phone rang.

He listened for a moment. "Gotcha."

Looking slightly less unsmiling, he stuffed the phone in his pocket. "David's copied pages have reached the office in Chicago."

"All *right*," Stephen said.

"Got a loose end to tie up—getting a search warrant to impound every piece of paper, weapon, and computer in the Boudreaux mansion. Then the FBI will have a little celebration of its own—and raise a glass of Bob Gallagher's favorite whiskey in his honor."

"Can we come?" Stephen asked.

"No. But they've got booze on the Internet too. I'll be in touch. Lot of paperwork." He went out the door.

The Bishop's wife returned with a dress. "Did you square dance with a barbed-wire fence?"

"Something like that."

"Let's take care of those cuts. I've got a poultice that might be just the thing." She led me to the bedroom.

The stuff smelled like sulfur and wintergreen. But darned if it didn't help.

When we came out, Stuart was setting the table for lunch.

"I owe you one, Carolyn," he said. "How'd you like a

brand new series to come out next year? Jennifer Jenner's getting on my nerves. When she hits puberty, it'll only get worse."

"Can I afford it?"

He set down the last platter. "I'll take half my usual advance."

I sat. "How about *no* advance? Seems like the least you could do."

He looked pained, then shrugged. "First manuscript due in six months."

"Make it three. My back's killing me."

"I thought owing the *Boudreauxs* was bad."

"I don't pull out authors' fingernails. Even though most of them deserve it."

* * *

After lunch we gathered our belongings from the barn and put them in a horse-drawn buggy. "This will take you to town," the Bishop said. "Godspeed." He and his wife went inside.

Aaron and I lingered by the barn. Farewells weren't so dramatic in the middle of the day, and the smell of manure didn't add to the ambiance.

"I never felt the need to go through Rumspringa," he said. "But if I had, I doubt it would have matched the last few weeks."

I pushed a little pile of straw with the toe of my shoe. "Think you'll ever leave?"

"Can't. We all have to be true to ourselves, don't we?"

I looked at the horse. He looked at me.

"Expected you'd say that. This is your path, and you have to follow it."

"Thank you for understanding."

I put my hands on my hips. "Think you'll ever see *Witness*, though? The movie, I mean."

He smiled. "Might. Have to work my way up to it, though. I could start with having a root beer next time I'm in town. Then maybe an actual *Mountain Dew*."

I laughed, but felt my eyes well up.

I kissed him on the cheek and watched him blush.

"Your steed and carriage await," he said.

EPILOGUE

THREE WEEKS LATER, DAVID ENTERED THE WITNESS protection program.

The Boudreaux family did have a high-powered lawyer, but not high enough. Angel was indicted for tax evasion and sentenced to 30 years in prison without parole. Ernie got five years. Nick got 40 for the murder of Robert Gallagher.

Jeremy was sentenced to life for assault and sundry killings. The Nameless Girl, who turned out to be April Byrd, got by with three years and probation.

Albert Treacher became the subject of a Court TV documentary, which led to an appearance on *Dancing with the Stars*, where he lasted two weeks before blowing out his knee.

Max Boudreaux, who had indeed suffered a stroke, died shortly after Angel went to jail. This time his funeral was not live-streamed.

Stuart joined Gamblers Anonymous. He also put Jennifer Jenner on hold and delivered the first book in his new series. It was Long Johns Silver, about a pirate with magic underwear and a parrot who could only meow. *Publishers Weekly* gave it a starred review, and sales made Jennifer look like *The Big Book of Shockingly Terrible Smells*.

Hunter's still a jerk.

Last I heard Aaron was engaged to that good Amish girl, Susanna. But he struggles with Mountain Dew addiction.

As for me—I'm doing fine, thank you.

Though I do dress up in my Amish outfit sometimes and throw together a little pan rabbit and a chicken pot pie.

JOHN WESLEY TUCKER IS NEITHER AN ORDINARY DETECTIVE NOR AN ORDINARY MAN.

Private Investigator John Wesley Tucker is hired to do a routine background check for a wealthy oil man, an aspiring politician. His investigation is complicated by his involvement in other cases and events which may be tied to a person associated with his client.

His partner, Christine, finds herself struggling to come to grips with her own ideals and beliefs. She and John are being followed by members of an unknown agency. When they learn there is a connection between the agency and Christine's former boss, all the disparate threads are woven together into a tapestry of death.

John and those around him will be led into a trap from which few will walk away.

A fast-paced, contemporary detective thriller with action, intrigue and a spiritual twist!

On Amazon Now

ABOUT THE AUTHOR

John Duckworth is a novelist, editor, playwright, scriptwriter, cartoonist, and father of twins. After earning his bachelor's degree at Linfield College, he spent 35 years in the publishing industry as a curmudgeonly editor, product developer, and author, working with people like Ken Blanchard, Dr. Kevin Leman, Richard Foster, and Calvin Miller, producers like VeggieTales, organizations like Focus on the Family and companies like Random House, Thomas Nelson, NavPress, Group Publishing, Zondervan and Rainfall Toys.

His works include *Joan 'n' the Whale, Just for a Moment I Saw the Light,* four collections of short plays, a ton of curriculum, at least 90 articles and short stories and three videos about a giant chipmunk puppet. He also contributed chapters to several trade books, edited scores of nonfiction and fiction titles, wrote animation and live action scripts for a major video series, several ounces of online content, and co-directed a traveling drama troupe called the Jericho Roadshow. On the radio he's done voice-over work for the popular *Adventures in Odyssey* program and wrote, directed, and performed in *The Semi-Amusing Half-Hour Comedy Show.*

After producing nearly 250 issues of weekly publications *Power for Living* and *FreeWay,* he created seven multi-volume series of youth ministry resources. He's edited or rewritten hundreds of books, articles, and lesson plans.

John's hobbies include figuring out how to promote himself while pretending to be humble, reading stories to children in the hospital, holding tiny babies in the neonatal intensive care unit, and feeding the cat. He and his lovely wife, Liz, live in Colorado Springs.

www.ingramcontent.com/pod-product-compliance
Lightning Source LLC
Chambersburg PA
CBHW011747010726
47498CB00012B/2968